Fake Dating the SEAL

ALOHA ROMANCE SERIES • BOOK TEN

CHRIS KENISTON

Indie House Publishing

Indie House Publishing

MORE BOOKS
By Chris Keniston

Honeysuckle Texas
Sweet Beginnings
Sweet Surprise
Sweet Temptation
Sweet Deal
Sweet Obsession
Sweet Tomorrows
Sweet Redemption

The Billionaire Barons of Texas
Just One Date
Just One Spark
Just One Dance
Just One Take
Just One Taste
Just One Shot
Just One Chance
Just One Mistake
Just One Family
Just One Rodeo
Just One Surprise
Just One Look

Hart Land Lakeside Inn
Heather
Lily
Violet
Iris
Hyacinth
Rose
Calytrix
Zinnia

Poppy
Picture Perfect

Farraday Country
Adam
Brooks
Connor
Declan
Ethan
Finn
Grace
Hannah
Ian
Jamison
Keeping Eileen
Loving Chloe
Morgan
Neil
Owen
Paxton
Quinn

Honeymoon Series
Honeymoon for One
Honeymoon for Three
Honeymoon for Four
Honeymoon for Five
Honeymoon for Six
Honeymoon for Seven

Aloha Romance Series:
Aloha Texas
Almost Paradise
Mai Tai Marriage
Dive Into You
Look of Love
Love by Design
Love Walks In
Shell Game
Flirting with Paradise
Fake Dating the SEAL

Surf's Up Flirts:
(Aloha Series Companions)
Shall We Dance
Love on Tap
Head Over Heels
Perfect Match
Just One Kiss
It Had to Be You
Cat's Meow

CHAPTER ONE

"What's that smell?" Sara Alani sniffed at the air like a bloodhound seeking its mark.

"My fritters!" Maile Everrett shouted from across the room. Bright red and purple and blue flowers from the family matriarch's neck to her toes flew past Sara. For the mother of four and grandmother to three of her grandchildren and even more almost grandchildren, that woman could move. Not to mention she wore a muumuu like no one else on the island.

"I've got it," a call came from the kitchen as Maile disappeared through the doorway. Emily Everrett Hamilton had come in the back door and reaching the oven minutes before her mother, averted a near disaster.

"Well." Maile slid the hot baking dish onto the stone trivet that always sat on the counter. For anyone who baked and cooked as often as Maile did, putting the thing away simply made no sense. "Only the row closest to the back of the oven are toast."

Reaching for one of the fritters with a darkened rim around the edge, Sara pulled her hand back and licked her burned finger.

"You know better than that." Maile grabbed the hand and shoved it under the cold water faucet, a move she'd done often when Sara and the Everrett girls would help in the family kitchen growing up.

Rabb, the family's beloved German shepherd, stood at his master's feet. Any other dog would have been waiting for a dropped treat, but Sara knew as well as anyone else in the kitchen, that the astute dog was more concerned for Maile's safety. As soon as the animal was convinced that

Maile's mad dash across the house and Sara's hand under running water was not a major, or even minor, crisis, he plopped to the ground from the corner of the room where he could oversee all the happenings.

The front door flew open and now the sweet chaos of the Everrett family was about to truly begin. Billy, the oldest child and only son, came through the door carrying their two year old son Eddie, named after the Everrett family patriarch who passed years ago from an unexpected heart attack. Billy's wife Angela had their daughter Isabella by the hand.

The four year old easily dragged her mother toward the kitchen. "Hurry, Mommy, cookie time."

On their tails, Nick Harper, who might as well have been an Everrett considering how close, like Sara, he'd been to the Everrett brood, ushered his own family—Maile's almost grandchildren—through the doorway.

Within minutes the kitchen was filled with giggling children and their parents all talking at the same time. Sara had to smile. Only once had she missed the annual Christmas cookie baking day at the Everrett household, and that was because she'd been confined to bed with strep throat. The memory broadened her smile. When she'd fully recovered she'd had Maile Everrett all to herself one afternoon after school and baked the best looking Santa and reindeer cookies ever. It hadn't been the same as the loving chaos of the whole family baking on that special day, but Maile had made it special for her nonetheless.

Even though Sara had wonderful loving parents, she always felt doubly blessed to have the Everretts as a second set of parents. Except of course for the matchmaking thing. Sara had spent the last six years trying to explain to her mother and her mother's best friend that she could find her own man—when she was ready. Whether the two women doubted her ability to find love or if she'd ever be ready, was a mystery to her. Especially since with the best of intentions, those two had tried to hook her up in one way or another with pretty much any breathing male old enough to order a beer for more years than she cared to think about.

"You doing okay?" Emily Everrett, her dearest friend since they'd met the first day of preschool and their mothers had become as fast friends as she and Emily, smiled at her. Ever since Emily turned thirty and she and Doug decided that it was time to start a family, Emily seemed to be more worried about Sara's biological clock than Sara. After all, she still had a few months until her own thirtieth birthday and in this day and age, thirty wasn't all that old for starting a family.

"You know I love cookie baking day." Sara smiled at Emily.

"I do." Her friend's eyes were filled with love, friendship, and, Sara feared, just a bit of pity.

"Don't you start turning into my mothers."

"Me?" Emily's eyes doubled in size. "What did I do?"

"Nothing. Yet." The minute Emily discovered she and Doug were having a baby, she'd tried to set Sara up with one of the dive shop customers who'd been getting certified to scuba dive. The guy had been nice enough, and handsome enough, but it hadn't taken long to figure out he had more interest in the fish than in women. Especially her.

"What are you two doing out here?" Apron tied around her waist, hands on her hips, Maile stood at the kitchen threshold. "It's time to mix the dough."

"Yes, ma'am." Emily saluted, even though unlike her brother and most of his buddies, she'd never been in the military.

As Sara passed by her friend's mother, Maile reached for hand and leaned in almost conspiratorially. Sara braced herself. She'd seen that look on Maile and her mother's faces too many times.

Lowering her voice, Maile glanced back into the kitchen as if worried someone would overhear her sharing state secrets, "Emily tells me there's a new teacher at the high school."

Sara nodded cautiously.

"He's not married."

And here they went again. Why did Christmas have to heighten everyone's interest in finding Sara a man? She loved the holidays but her family's need to find her a match always seemed to dampen the joy. A few years they were downright miserable. She'd been nudged under the mistletoe with men who had as little interest in kissing her as she had in kissing them. Maybe it was time she tried in earnest to find a man on her own. Too bad she couldn't ask Santa.

This was it. Terminal leave. Three months paid vacation, and then Senior Chief SEAL Kenny Yates, a respected and battle tested leader, would officially be a civilian. "Mr. Yates." Kenny let the words roll around on his tongue. Granted, he'd been called that often enough in the real world, but no one would be addressing him as Chief—ever again. He wouldn't be leading any more teams, and he wouldn't be doing any more battles. At least not the life or death kind.

The wheels of the commercial jet touched down on the Kona runway. For the first time since his paperwork for intent to separate was approved by the chain of command, he felt at ease. Kona had a way of doing that. Though he suspected without the warmth of the Everrett family and his former Navy buddies now working at the dive shop, Kona would be just another beach.

At the last United States airport where passengers descended the stairs to an open tarmac from a commercial jet, he got his first breath of Hawaiian retirement standing in the open doorway. Just a little bit longer and he'd unpack his carryon at the hotel. A smile pulled at the corners of his mouth. He'd decided at the last minute to book a room at the swankiest resort on the island. Normally, he'd stay with Billy when he came to the Big Island, but this time, he wanted just a few days to get his bearings. He'd told his friend of many years that he'd be arriving today, and would reach out tomorrow. After an hour of back and forth debate over whether or not he should save his money, Billy finally caved and agreed a few days of posh pampering might not be such a bad thing. He hoped his friend was right.

Making a beeline for the taxis, within minutes of landing, he was pulling up to the Kings Resort. Though the resort was originally named after the famed King Kamehameha, it wasn't long before the powers that be figured out the simpler name, Kings, was much easier for tourists and travel agents to manage. Still, the statue of the Hawaiian leader in yellow and red greeted him by the front drive. He just wished he'd felt a bit more like home. Maybe once he figured out where he was going to live he'd feel more settled. Despite having had months to think about where to drop anchor, he hadn't been able to decide if he should stay on the island, or go back stateside to where he grew up. He might not have any family left in his hometown, but he still had friends and memories. And yet, much of the time, Kona felt more like home even if he hadn't lived here as a kid. Which probably explained why he was having such a hard time making up his mind. Bottom line, he simply wasn't ready to make that decision. Not yet.

"Mr. Yates. Welcome." The pretty brunette behind the check in counter smiled up at him. "We have you in the luau suite."

"Suite?"

Her gaze lifted from the keyboard. "Yes, sir. You've been upgraded."

Not being a member of any loyalty programs, he had no clue how this had come to happen.

His prolonged silence must have spoken volumes of what was on his mind because the brunette smiled a little wide. "Our manager is former Navy. I believe someone mentioned that you're retiring." She blinked. "Thank you for your service."

As he always did when someone approached him to thank him for doing his job, he nodded and smiled back. Taking the keycard and room number, he tapped his toe behind him and did a perfect military turn. That was one habit he was going to have to work on breaking.

No sooner had he closed the door to his suite behind him, when his phone buzzed. A text from Billy. *Did Mom's gift arrive?*

Kenny scanned the room, but it only took a second to find what Billy most likely referred to. A massive plate of homemade Christmas cookies. His cheeks tugged hard at the corners of his mouth. There were few things in this world as delicious as Maile Everrett's homemade holiday cookies. He suspected that the love in that family had to be the secret ingredient.

Phone in hand, he shoved one in his mouth and began to tap out a response. *Shortbread. My favorite. Tell her thank you.*

Tell her yourself. You're expected for dinner tomorrow night.

Of course he was. Laughing to himself, he tapped at the phone again. *Wouldn't miss it.*

Already he felt a thousand times better than he had when he'd gotten on the flight from Honolulu. Shoving the curtains open, he took in the expansive view. The nice thing about being in the Navy was that most bases were somewhere near an ocean. Even though he'd grown up in suburbia, he'd always felt most at home near a body of water.

The low moonlight shone on the rippling waves. So very peaceful. For the first time since deciding to separate from Uncle Sam's Navy, he was going to simply enjoy the view. He wasn't going to think about what came next, or if he'd made the right decision, or if he'd simply lost his mind. Sliding the room card into his wallet, he cranked the window open just enough for a breeze and turned to find the rooftop bar. Figuring out the rest of his life could wait another day.

CHAPTER TWO

How could so few people go through so many towels? Sara shoved the door to the restroom lounge area open with her hip and stacked the fresh pile of crisp white hand towels on the marble counter. One by one, she carefully folded each one and stacked them into what, appropriately for the season, reminded her of a Christmas Tree.

The season was the key reason why she accepted working the late shift attendant's slot. Working the day shift in housekeeping had been steady work for years, and every so often, one of the guests would leave her a nice fat tip for making their beds and straightening their rooms. Sometimes she thought the people who stayed at the Kings Resort had more money than Croesus. But it was the restroom attendants that got the plum tips. Always working alone, there was no pooling and sharing of tips. Whatever a patron gave her was all hers. The first time a hulking pro ball player had given her a hundred-dollar tip for simply handing him a small towel after he'd washed his hands, had sold her on taking the extra duty any time offered. The moonlighting had done wonders to help pad her bank account the last few years. Especially since what little she'd saved before moving home had been spent on that deadbeat boyfriend she'd supported until she couldn't stand it anymore. Even if it had meant moving home under her mother's watchful eye. Now she was saving for her own home, no more renting, something that couldn't be taken away from her. Unfortunately, Hawaii wasn't known for bargain real estate, so she might be saving for a lot longer than she'd like.

Taking a seat in the corner by the long wall of sinks, she

stared at the furnishings in the foyer. The idea of a foyer to the men's and ladies room was something she hadn't even considered before coming to work here. Though the sinks were along one wall, a door to the left led to the ladies room and across the way, a door to the men's room. But in between, in true five star luxury, the lounge had plush chairs and sofas, low coffee and side tables, fresh floral arrangements that would knock the socks off the florist for Buckingham Palace, as well as vanity areas for women to touch up their faces or hair. It was also her responsibility to offer them perfume, hand lotion, or any other personal care item the hotel provided. Same for the men, but few cared how they looked when they came out from taking a leak as long as their zipper was up.

The rooftop lounge, which had been buzzing with life an hour ago, was now down to a handful of stragglers. Checking her watch, at close to midnight, it would only be a little longer until her shift would be over. All she could think of for the last hour was getting a late snack and crawling under the covers and sleeping until the party at Maile Everrett's tomorrow afternoon, but an uneven clicking sound from inside the ladies room side of the restrooms caught her attention. The bathrooms had been empty when she'd gone to retrieve more towels and she hadn't heard anything before now. That was odd. Most women didn't spend that much time on the toilet. Not that it was any of her business.

The sound returned. The clicking louder. Not the even paces of a woman in heels, but an awkward arrangement of heavy and soft taps on the tile floor. Could the woman be dancing? Warring with the need to see what was going on and the responsibility of staying at her post, a loud thud followed by a squeal had Sara rushing into the ladies room to find a blonde woman with a sparkly dress and a very expensive-looking handbag on the marble floor, her back against the stall door. Her mascara smudged, her legs sprawled out from under her, she giggled happily at nothing in particular.

Carefully   kneeling   beside   the   woman,   the

overwhelming scent of tequila and coconut smacked Sara in the face. "Ma'am, are you okay?"

"I'm perfectly fine." The woman tried to wave dismissively but nearly toppled sideways. "Just resting."

"Let me help you up." Sara slipped an arm around the woman's waist and tried to lift her. The blonde was sheer dead weight, and the moment Sara got her halfway vertical, her knees buckled.

"Whee!" The blonde giggled as she slid back down.

Where were those pro ball players when you needed them? Heaving a deep sigh, Sara studied the woman still giggling at nothing in particular, and a strappy stiletto heel swinging like a pendulum from her finger. Sara glanced at the woman's feet—only one shoe. That would explain the odd tapping sound.

"Come on, let's try again to get you standing." Sara debated taking off the other shoe, but opted to just get the woman off the floor first, out of the toilets, and in the lounge they could deal with her footwear.

"You're so nice." The woman patted Sara's cheek with a clammy hand. "I like you. You smell good."

"Thank you." Steeling herself for another try, Sara looped her arms around the woman's waist, turned her face sideways to avoid the overpowering smell of tequila… and maybe *rum*? No wonder the woman couldn't walk. Squatting and then tugging with all her might, Sara was sure this time she'd get the woman to her feet when the blonde lurched forward and Sara's feet scrambled out from under her.

The wiggly woman squealed with the delight of a kid on a roller coaster and Sara flipped backward, the hundred pounds of blonde landing splat on top of her, knocking her breath out. Oh, this was so not good.

Kenny drained the last of his drink and set the glass on the polished bar top. After months of debriefings and paperwork, his mind still whirred with the ingrained routines of twenty years of military life. The rooftop had been exactly what he needed—the peaceful Kona night, the ocean breeze, a decent drink, and the distant sound of the waves went a long way to quiet the noise in his mind. A few more days of this and he'd be ready to take on his new world.

The bartender was wiping down glasses and putting them one by one in the rack below, clearly ready to close up shop. Only two tables remained occupied. One with a couple who wouldn't have noticed if a bomb landed beside them. He didn't doubt they'd be off to their room soon enough. At the other table, a single man with a glass in front of him and an empty one across the table told Kenny the guy hadn't been alone all night.

Taking out his wallet, he left a generous tip on the bar, and grinned to himself, thinking about the massive plate of Maile's shortbread cookies waiting for him in his room. The one thing that hadn't changed about coming to Kona was the warm, loving embrace of the Everrett family.

Tired from the long flight, and the single bourbon he'd drunk, he craved a walk on the beach followed by a good and long night's sleep, but first a quick detour to the men's room.

As he got closer to the restrooms, an odd noise drew his attention. It wasn't a scream or a cry for help, nothing that would set off an alarm in his gut, but it was…off. Hand on the men's room door, he waited another minute. A soft "oomph" followed by a low "humph," like someone struggling could easily be heard. Cocking his head, he debated if the noises could be someone in need, or someone trying to join the mile high club without an airplane. After a long few beats of silence, he pushed on the men's room door when a loud, startled shriek followed by a definitive *thud* had him freezing in place again.

That was a noise he recognized. It was the sound of a human body hitting the ground hard, and a feminine squeal that could mean anything from playful to terrified. He had no business going into the women's restroom, and his civilian brain was already telling him to turn back and mind his own business, but his instincts—the part of him that was still a SEAL, still a protector—overruled the logical part of his brain. Something was wrong.

Shoving the door open he took one hurried step, not surprised to find a huddle of human flesh on the floor. A flash of red hair splayed across the floor caught his eye first, followed by a blur of sparkles, and then arms and legs moving with groans and grunts. A cat fight or... "Excuse me."

The pair of tanned arms pressed from underneath against the sparkly dress stilled. A face covered by strands of long blonde hair that seemed to belong to the woman in the sparkling dress turned part way to see him. "Don't just stand there. Help get her off of me."

Now the picture was beginning to make more sense to him. "Sorry," he rushed the few steps and carefully grasped the blonde woman under her arms. "I'm going to lift her. Just lie still."

"Oh, hello there, handsome," the blonde slurred, her head lolling toward Kenny as he lifted her. "Are you my knight in shining armor?"

"Something like that." Kenny got her upright, though she immediately started to sway. "Easy there."

The blonde unexpectedly flung herself forward, and the next thing he knew, she stood on spaghetti legs with her arms wrapped around him. Inches away from his face, the smell of rum, and tequila, and who knew what else, almost overwhelmed him. Struggling to focus, the woman smiled wildly. "Hi."

"Careful." The woman from the floor now stood, glancing down as she straightened her uniform and brushed off any signs of struggle. "That one's like Velcro."

At least the redhead, that he now realized was a hotel employee, had a sense of humor. Only problem, now the blonde was indeed stuck to him like Velcro.

"Allie. What the hell is taking so long?" a deep male voice, probably the lone guy at the table for two, called from the lounge area.

"Hiiiii, Bradley." The blonde's breath could knock a man over. Her weight shifted and Kenny had to wrap an arm around her to stop her from falling on the floor—again.

The door squeaked and a man's head peered through the slight opening, his gaze landing on the three people before widening like a drunk owl. "What the hell."

Before Kenny could say a word, the man lunged forward, arm swinging and any other man would have been cold cocked. Despite the dead weight in his arms, Kenny managed to shift left, dip his torso and avoid the blow without dropping the woman.

The man wasn't so lucky. Momentum had him stumbling forward before finding his balance.

"Hey," the redhead yelled, turned so her back was to Kenny, her arm straight out pointing to the door, she stood between him and the drunk. "No men in the ladies room."

So the woman had a sense of humor *and* guts. She was actually trying to protect him. When was the last time someone—other than his teammates—tried to protect *him*?

"I suggest instead of starting trouble, the two of you get out of here and go home."

"We live in Jersey." The woman hiccupped, her hand flying to her mouth. "It's our," hiccup, "honeymoon."

"Fine." The redhead hadn't moved an inch. "Congratulations. Now leave."

"Come on, baby." The man moved toward his wife, slipping his arm around her waist until she leaned against him instead of Kenny.

"You may want to take off the other shoe." The redhead pointed at the heel still on the woman's foot and the other one still hooked on her finger.

The husband nodded, holding onto his wife as she fumbled with sliding the shoe off, and then the two wobbled out the door together.

Watching their backs until the bathroom door eased shut behind them, Kenny just shook his head. "Wonder what the odds are that they'll make it all the way to their room." He spun around to face the feisty redhead. "Sara?"

CHAPTER THREE

"**K**enny?" Sara blinked at him. Kenny Yates. Billy's friend, one of many SEALs who'd come to the island for visits through the years. They'd shared a few polite greetings from time to time, but for the most part he was always with the other men—friends, SEALs, the EOD guys—an entourage of muscle, quiet confidence, and lots and lots of testosterone.

"The one and only." He smiled. "Are things always this… entertaining around here?"

"Hardly," she practically snorted. "Usually the most excitement I have is when someone barfs in the toilet and misses. Then I get to clean up the mess. I don't usually get to pick up the drunk. Not that I did a very good job with her tonight."

"Hey, don't sell yourself short. I've got nearly a hundred pounds of muscle on you and she almost knocked me over."

"If they keep drinking like that, this honeymoon will be nothing but a blur for those two."

Kenny chuckled. He had a nice smile. Nice eyes too. Funny, she'd never noticed before. Then again, she'd probably been so hell bent on not giving her mother or her friends any reason to try and play matchmaker with a SEAL that she'd kept her head down and made herself scarce whenever any of Nick and Billy's buddies were in town. Heck, they'd even tried to fix her up with Doug back in the day, even though any fool could see he had it bad for Billy's sister Emily.

"So I gather drunken honeymooners aren't the normal clientele around here?"

"Nope. Lots of money though. No one wants to ruin their thousand dollar shoes or custom made Italian suits. A few folks may be a little tipsy, but falling down drunk like that…" She shook her head. "Thankfully, not very often." Needing something to do, she straightened her uniform again, took a quick look around to make sure everything was in order, then glanced up at Kenny. "Well, it's been interesting, but I don't want to keep you from whoever you're with."

"I'm not with anyone."

"You're here alone?" That was not what she expected. Most of Billy and Nick's single buddies from the Navy always had a girl, or more, hanging around them.

His chuckle deepened. "Don't sound so surprised. It's my first night back in Kona and I wanted a few days to decompress in a little luxury."

"The antithesis of the military," she teased.

He tapped the tip of his nose. "Bingo."

Sara's stomach chose that second to rumble. Loudly. "Excuse me. All I had between shifts was a bag of trail mix."

"That's not much."

She shrugged and forced a smile. "The Kings Hotel frowns on attendants dining in their restroom lounges."

"When does your shift end?"

Flipping her wrist, she glanced at the time. "Fifteen minutes ago."

"Good." His smile spread. "I was going to grab a snack and take a walk on the beach. If you're not too tired, I'd enjoy the company."

Tonight was definitely a night for the unexpected. She didn't expect to pick up an extra shift. She didn't expect to be tackled by a drunk. And she most definitely did not expect to be invited for a walk on the beach with a handsome SEAL. Her gaze dropped to her uniform.

"I'm sure no one will care what you're wearing."

Her head still bent to glance down, only her eyes lifted to meet his. Was he a mind reader as well as strong and handsome?

"If you want to change, I can wait."

Lifting her chin, she tipped her head slightly. Was she that easy to read? Tonight had definitely been one for the record books. If she was smart, she'd run the other way. Nothing good ever came from a walk in the moonlight along the shore with handsome military men. It just didn't. Then again, her life wasn't exactly filled with anything even a little bit interesting or different. What the hell, one night out with a friendly SEAL couldn't really hurt. Straightening, she nodded. "No one cares what I'm wearing. Especially not at this hour. If you don't care that I'm in uniform, neither do I."

"Good. Where should we go?"

Now that was a completely different problem. Plenty of bars were still open for another hour or so, but nothing *on* the beach. "I have an idea. Follow me." Leading the way out of the restrooms, she paused at the bar where the bartender was almost finished cleaning up. "Hey, Steve."

"Long night?"

"You wouldn't believe." She rolled her eyes. "Can we have a couple of bottles of water." She spun around to face Kenny. "Would you prefer a soft drink or beer?"

He shook his head. "Water is perfect."

After waving good night to Steve and thanking him for the drinks, they proceeded to the service elevator. Kenny's gaze took in every detail along the way. He carefully read the sign posted about *Employees Only* just before silently following her onto the elevator. On the ground floor she made her way to the kitchen where the night crew was prepping for the morning menus. Another few minutes and one of her friends in the kitchen had packed them a boxed lunch. "If I were a guest, we could eat this on the veranda. They don't bring in the tables at night."

"I'm a guest. Can't you join me?"

When he'd said he wanted to decompress in luxury, she'd thought he meant this evening at the rooftop bar. She didn't realize he'd meant that he'd checked in.

Her head bobbed. "I can."

This time, she followed him out onto the lanai, and

almost blushed when he pulled her chair out for her. How long had it been since she'd been on a date with anyone who had manners? Not that this was a date, but still, it was nice to be treated like a lady, the way all her military friends treated their wives and sisters. She slid one of the boxed meals in front of him. "Not sure what's in it, but I can guarantee you, whatever it is, it will be delicious."

Kenny unwrapped a sandwich, set his napkin on his lap, and took a big bite. "Oh, my. This is a *seriously* delicious sandwich."

"The hotel has their own secret mayonnaise recipe."

"Works for me."

Forgetting her own food, she watched Kenny eating as if he hadn't been fed a decent meal in ages. Of course, being a SEAL he was probably used to rations or some such thing. Sucking in a slow deep breath, she wondered if she would look totally ridiculous if she simply sat here and watched the big handsome sailor eat.

Beyond content, Kenny polished off the last bite of his sandwich and leaned back in his chair. He wasn't sure if it was the bread, the chicken, or that secret mayonnaise Sara had mentioned that had made the sandwich taste so good. "That was excellent." He crumpled his napkin and set it in the empty box. "Your friend in the kitchen knows what they're doing."

"You won't get an argument out of me." Gently dabbing the corners of her mouth, she set her napkin on the box.

The simple contrast in gestures made him feel a bit like an uncouth buffoon. Maybe he'd spent too long living with men who scarf down their food, peed on the side of the road, and took pride in who could belch the loudest.

She heaved a gentle sigh, and blinked longer than she should have.

"Hey, it's late. You've had a long day. We can skip the

walk if you need to hit the sack."

"Nah. I'm off tomorrow and can sleep as late as I want. Besides, when I'm this tired, a nice walk in the fresh air will help me sleep."

"If you're sure?"

"Sure." That smile was as brilliant as the Hawaii stars above.

Gathering up the remnants of their impromptu dinner, he tossed it into a nearby trash can, then followed her to the wide steps that led to the sandy beach. Pausing at the edge of the patio by the low wall, Sara kicked off her shoes, tucking them neatly to one side of the stairs. Kenny did the same.

The sound of waves grew louder as they approached the water's edge. At this hour the beach was deserted, nothing but moonlight reflecting off the gentle surf. It was nice to be at the beach simply to enjoy the serenity. No mission objectives, no timeline to meet, no team depending on him to make the right call. Just sand, water, and the company of an interesting woman.

"So," he slowed his pace to match her stride, "do you work a lot of double shifts?"

Her shoulders lifted in a gentle shrug. "Not really, but I hardly ever turn one down if it comes up."

"All work and no play isn't good for a soul."

"Neither is starving."

His steps faltered. "Am I missing something?"

"Sorry," she chuckled. "I suppose that was a tad overly dramatic."

"Only if you're not on the verge of being homeless."

"No." She shook her head. "I live with my parents."

"Ah." He was beginning to see the bigger picture.

"At first I thought it would just be for a little bit while I got back on my feet after kicking Vinny to the curb. But soon I realized, on my wages, even with tips, I'd be renting and living from paycheck to paycheck for the rest of my life if I didn't get some savings."

"So you're saving to buy a house?"

Her face lit up again. He liked it when she smiled. "I

am, a cozy cottage with a yard for a vegetable garden and lush flowers I can cut and place in vases to keep the inside smelling as sweet as the outdoors." Her excitement suddenly dimmed. "But Hawaii isn't exactly the home of bargain real estate. And then every so often something happens that forces me to dip into the savings. Usually it's my car."

"A clunker?"

"No. Just getting on in years. Sort of like gravity and an old woman."

That made him laugh a little louder.

"How about you?" She shifted her attention from the beach ahead and glanced at him. "Plan to buy a house some day, or already own one?"

"I actually do own a small house. In California. I fell into a sweet deal when I was stationed there, then when I moved on, I decided to keep it. I mostly rent it to other military personnel. So far it's worked out well."

"So you plan to settle down some day in California?"

"Not some day. In a few months I'll be free to settle anywhere I want, I just don't think it's California."

"Where do you want to go?"

That was the same question he'd been asking himself since he put in his retirement papers. He'd been in the military moving from place to place for so long, he was ready for a home. That much he was sure of. The only thing close to family he had were the Everretts, but that didn't mean settling here was the answer. California was a nice house, but not a home. So he was still circling the same question. "I'm not sure."

Silent, they walked a bit further, taking in the sound of the waves rolling ashore and the gentle breeze on their faces.

"Is there a man in your life?" He couldn't believe he'd just asked that. It was none of his business, but curiosity had gotten the best of him.

"You mean a boyfriend?" She shook her head before he could answer. "I've been on a few dates here and there since Vinny, but nothing serious. You might say once burned, twice shy. I suppose eventually I'll be ready to find someone. I just wish everyone would stop feeling sorry for me."

"I didn't mean to—"

"Oh," she stopped to face him, her eyes wide, "I really meant my mother and Maile."

"Billy's mom?"

She nodded, and looking straight ahead again, continued walking.

"What do they do?"

"You mean besides try to match me up with every and any eligible bachelor on the island?"

His mind ran through all his visits to the island. A vague memory tickled the back of his thoughts. "Didn't they set you up once with Doug?"

"They tried."

He squinted, turning his mind back in time. "And John Maplewood?"

Her head bobbed. "Yeah, they tried that too. And now even Emily is getting in on the 'poor Sara' mindset."

Kenny studied her profile in the moonlight. Red hair catching the silver light, intelligent eyes, easy laugh, and the kind of straightforward personality that made conversation effortless. "I don't understand. Why poor Sara? You're smart, have a good sense of humor, and are a total knockout."

Looking at him, surprise flickering across her face. "Thank you. That's... actually really nice to hear."

"It's the truth." He shrugged. "Their matchmaking efforts seem like a solution in search of a problem."

"Well. Regardless." Sara stopped walking and turned to face him. "I love Mom, and Maile's been like a second mother to me, but sometimes I feel smothered by their efforts. Especially this time of year."

"Why this time of year?"

She shrugged and returned to walking. "I think around the holidays, they think that everyone should have someone to kiss under the mistletoe."

"Well, it is nice not to be standing alone on New Year's

Eve watching all the happy couples ringing in the New Year with their lips locked while you fold yourself into a corner."

Her face tipped up at him. "At least you weren't forced to go to that party with someone your mother picked for you."

Now he laughed. "No. And for the record, I don't go to many New Year's Eve parties. Most of the time I've been deployed somewhere. Heck, half the time I didn't even realize it was New Year's Eve."

"I'm sorry."

"Why? I don't regret my twenty years of service. I made a choice. I married the Navy. It wouldn't have been fair to leave a wife behind to worry about me three hundred days a year or more. Or to be home alone on New Year's Eve watching the ball drop, wishing she had someone to kiss under the mistletoe."

"I've heard that before. You're not the only military man who feels that way." Glancing over her shoulder at the resort in the distance, she turned. "We should head back."

"Yeah, it's getting late."

By the time they made their way back to the resort, Kenny realized he'd been more relaxed in the past hour than he'd been in months. No military protocols to follow, no life-or-death decisions to make, just a pleasant conversation with a woman who seemed to actually enjoy his company for its own sake.

"This was nice," Sara reached for their shoes. "Thank you for the food and the walk."

"Thank you for the company. And for not letting me get punched by a drunk husband in the women's bathroom."

Sara laughed. "That would have been tough to explain to hotel security."

For a moment he felt like an awkward teen at his date's front door. Shaking the image from his mind, he took a step in retreat, and smiled. "I'll probably see you again at at the Everretts?"

"Absolutely." She smiled. "Sleep well, sailor."

"You too." He watched her turn and walk away. Heading back inside, he muttered to himself, "Why the heck did Mrs. Everrett think that woman needed a matchmaker?"

CHAPTER FOUR

"Hurry up. We don't want to be late."

For once, Sara agreed with her mother. Today was her favorite day of the season, aside from Christmas itself of course. For as long as she could remember the Everrett family and closest of friends would gather to put up the Christmas tree and then decorate it. By evening, half the island would be at their home to turn on the lights, and enjoy the mother of all pot luck dinners. The intrusive matchmaking usually didn't happen for a few more weeks. Then she'd be bombarded with a parade of eligible bachelors, most of whom she wouldn't have picked if they'd been the last men on earth. Trying to walk and slip into her new sandals at the same time, she hobbled into the living room. "Ready."

"It might be easier if you sat down to do that."

Tugging the strap in place, Sara straightened to her full height. "No need. Done and ready." Keys dangling from her finger, she waved them at her mother. "Let's go."

Her mother was already out the front door and waiting on the porch, a massive tray of Mexican lasagna in her hands. Ever since her mother discovered this recipe of noodles with Mexican seasoned meats and cheeses instead of marinara sauce and mozzarella, this was her go-to pot luck contribution.

By the time they pulled up to the Everrett home, Billy's truck was in front, the massive evergreen tree on the roof and at least a half a dozen men surrounding the vehicle, each shouting instructions to the other. Sara had to laugh. As entertaining as watching her friends lob witty retorts and occasional digs, she knew that when these men served together, they operated as a very well oiled machine. Which was probably why they hadn't lost a tree yet.

"Need a hand?" Sara shot Billy a fat grin. "You know, from a girl?" She couldn't help teasing him.

"That's right." Hands on her hips, Maille stood on the front stoop. "If you bunch of galoots don't get that tree in the house and put up, I'm going to have the girls do it."

Mumbles and grumbles could be heard coming from the truck as they finally coordinated their efforts and had the thing on its way inside the house.

When Kenny came past her, hanging on to the trunk of the tree with Billy and the others, dispersed from bottom to tip bearing the weight of the massive evergreen, he winked at her.

The action caught Sara off guard. He'd never done that before. Then again, they'd never wrestled a drunken bride together before either. Before she could do much more than smile at the man, she turned and spotted Maile still on the stoop, a sly grin on her face. "Uh oh." Almost afraid, she glanced over her shoulder. Sure enough, her mom was eyeing Maile and the two women had mirror grins on their faces. Oh, how Sara hoped those dazzling smiles were over a great tree and had nothing to do with the way Kenny had sort of greeted her.

In the house, the normal chaos that came with this day of the year was in full swing. Boxes containing ornaments were piled along one wall. Maile and Ava each removed the lids, and slid a box toward the middle. Across the way, Nick and Kara were opening the boxes of lights, handing them off to Doug and Billy who seemed to be on lights duty. Off to the side, carrying a large tote labeled Father Christmas, Kenny set it down in the next room, one by one removing Maile's collection of vintage Santas that reminded Sara of the Ghost of Christmas Past.

Every year, new little ones joined the escapades. Seeing Emily playing with her nephew Eddie made Sara smile pretty wide herself. From the moment Em had shared with her that they were expecting their first child, Sara was over the moon for her best friend. In fact, she was so happy for her friend, anyone would think Sara was the one about to start a family. Emily was such a fantastic school teacher that Sara knew her friend would be an amazing mom.

Moving closer to Maile and Ava, Sara reached for one of the boxes of ornaments and Maile waved a hand at her, shaking her head. "We've got this. You go help with my Santas and Angels. Men have terrible eyes for decoration."

Fighting the urge to roll her eyes. Sara smiled and nodded and turned toward the other room. She was going to have to explain—once again—to her mother and her mother's best friend, that she could find her own man.

"Hi," a voice that felt as smooth as velvet and deep as the ocean floated over her.

"I've been sent to supervise."

Kenny raised one dark brow. "Supervise?"

"Translation—the mothers want us to work together."

His brows folded into a deep V before quickly arching high on his forehead with understanding. "We've been targeted."

"Not we," she rolled her eyes for real this time, "you. They've set their sights on you. My suspicion is after all these years, they no longer care that you're a little older than me. You winked at me; in their minds, we're as good as married with two point two kids and a dog. I'm sorry."

"No need to apologize." He handed her the first large doll with it's flowing velvet robe and fur collar, really did look like the Ghost of Christmas Past from the old Christmas Carol movie. "I think it's kind of sweet how much they care for you. Which means I'm going to consider it a compliment they think I'm good enough for you."

"Sorry to burst your bubble, but anyone with the right chromosomes and no wedding ring would rank on their list of matches."

"Ouch." He handed her a smaller doll that was designed to sit on a ledge.

Looking around at her options, she decided to walk it over to the mantel.

"When I found that in a little shop in England, I thought of Maile. If I'd been hunting for the perfect gift I probably would never have found it, shopping is not my strength, but that doll just jumped out at me." His smile showed the pride he felt at having given the Everrett matriarch a treasured gift.

Now she understood why this particular decoration was one of Maile's favorites. When Maile had told her eons ago that it was a gift, Sara had assumed it was from one of her kids. She should have realized that as far as Maile was concerned, all her children's friends—in and out of the military—were like her own children and the gift could have come from any one of them.

They'd succeeded in emptying two of the boxes when Ava came to help. By the time all the Santa, angels, and Father Christmas dolls were on display through out the family room, and a few in strategic places around the social areas of the house, the men in the other room were down to the last string of lights. Nick on his knees testing light bulbs, Doug standing a few feet from his brother-in-law with a fully lit string of lights hanging around his neck and extended in each arm, while Billy squatted low, meticulously connecting each bulb on the bottom branches.

When the three men eased back to admire their handy work, the whole room erupted in applause. The tree reached the ceiling and sparkled with an array of bright colors that danced across the walls. Having a pre-lit artificial tree was a heck of a lot easier, but the old fashioned bulbed strings of light in multi colors, carefully wrapped around the freshly cut tree could not be beat. She absolutely loved it. Now all she had to do was help with the ornament hanging and steer clear of all the single men in the place. Maybe her mother and Maile would give up on the matchmaking efforts. She blew out a sigh. And maybe she'd win the Irish Sweepstakes.

"Now what can I do?" Kenny came to stand next to Maile Everrett. He'd done his best to avoid Sara. Not that he didn't enjoy her company, or appreciate another opportunity to sit and chat, but he also knew all too well that if given even a hint of interest, her mother and Billy's mother would be plotting to hook the two of them up. While that wouldn't be such a horrible thing, he did have quite a few years on Sara and knew that the older women's efforts embarrassed Sara, so he did his best to keep his distance from her.

"Here." Maile handed him a huge plate of raw kabobs. "Take these to Doug by the grill." Running the kitchen like a Marine on a mission, she turned to Angela by the fridge. "The mango salad is on the bottom shelf."

Turning on his heel, Kenny carried the kabobs across the lawn and found himself scanning for Sara. He hoped she was doing okay. The thought of the older women's matchmaking efforts upsetting Sara had him a bit unsettled.

On the rear lawn, along with wickets for a game of croquet at one end and a volleyball net at the other, every space in between was taken up with an array of six foot tables decorated with Santa at the beach plastic tablecloths. At the far back, to the west of the grill, the rear property wall was backdrop to table after table of food, and with every new guest arriving, more food came with them. The Everrett family holiday potluck to kick off the season had gotten bigger and bigger every year. Pretty soon, the family was going to have to rent a hall to keep up with the crowds.

"Here." Maile walked up to him as he approached the patio doors, a massive bowl of mustard potato salad in her hands. "Set this on the table with the other salads, please."

"Yes, ma'am." He almost saluted, but caught himself in time.

Her smile warmed. For a moment, she was out of drill sergeant mode and in substitute mother mode. "Such a nice boy."

Laughter almost burst forth from deep in his gut. He was almost forty years old. It had been an awfully long time since anyone had referred to him as a boy. Still, all he could think to say was, "Thank you."

"Okay. Shoo. Go take the bowl, then serve yourself a plate and take a seat. We need to get the food lines going before my refrigerator explodes from over stuffing."

This time he nodded, did as he'd been told, and had a dish piled high with pulled pork, salads, breads, and the wonderful kabobs. He'd barely made it halfway across the lawn when this time he was intercepted by Sara's mother. "Please have a seat at table nine. I'm trying to get everyone to spread out a bit."

His gaze drifted to the tables before him, settling on number nine. An empty table with few people at any of the surrounding tables. "Sure thing." He nodded and smiled back at her.

No more than a few minutes had passed when Maile Everrett appeared, practically dragging Sara behind her. "Here, you should sit. It will encourage more people to stop huddling by the food tables and take seats." The woman wasn't content with directing Sara to the same table as him, she yanked a chair out from beside him and gestured to Sara. "Not there. Here."

Sara already had a hand on the back of the seat across from him. When Maile insisted she surrender her chair to sit beside him, for a long moment, her eyes closed and he wondered if she was praying. Plastering on a wide forced smile, she nodded and worked around the table to sit beside him.

Content with her work, Maile bobbed her head, patted Sara on the shoulder, and walked toward the house.

"I really am sorry." Her fork dangling in front of her, she stared at the food not him.

"Nothing to be sorry for."

Letting the fork drop to the plate, she shifted to face him. "Yes there is, they've set their sites on you. If you're lucky they'll give up quickly and move on to someone else."

"Someone else?"

She nodded.

"Anyone in particular?"

"Oh, who knows." She heaved a deep, frustrated sigh. "I really thought they'd given up on you years ago."

"I beg your pardon?" He wasn't sure quite how to take that.

His response must have been perfect because the tension in her shoulders eased and a real smile teased her lips. "I mean, on matching you up with me. They love you."

"And I love them." He took a second to scan all the people in the yard. Some he knew, some he didn't, but there were many he loved very much. Including Maile Everrett. Returning his gaze to Sara, he tipped his head. "They're really going to keep making you sit next to strangers until you find Mr. Right."

"Mr. Right would be nice, but after all their failed efforts, I'm convinced they'd be happy with Mr. Good Enough."

"I can't believe that. I've never known anyone in the Everrett family to settle. Ever."

"Okay. So, maybe I'm just a bit cynical." At that moment her gaze drifted toward the house and he knew the second she'd spotted what he had. Her mother and Maile were standing in the doorway, staring at them, smiling, hands waving back and forth, clearly delighted and he suspected it had nothing to do with the smorgasbord they'd set up.

"You don't suppose they're just happy with the turn out."

Sara spun to face him, one brow arched high, her glare was piercing.

"Okay. Maybe not." He looked at the two women with their heads together, giggling like school girls. An idea tickled the back of his brain. Could it work? Was it crazy? Would it help Sara? He couldn't think of a negative. It's not like she was a dog, and what did it matter she was younger. A decade ago yes, but now…. What the heck. "Sara Alani, would you be my date for the season?"

CHAPTER FIVE

Momentarily confused, Sara looked down at the drink Maile had given her and wondered if maybe it was more than just fruit punch. Sniffing at the glass, she didn't smell liquor. Maybe she merely misunderstood. Leveling her eyes to meet his waiting gaze, she took a breath. "I'm sorry. Say that again?"

He chuckled and leaned in, his gaze momentarily darting over his shoulder to where Maile and Mrs. Alani stood watching. Placing his hand over hers, he leaned even closer. "Don't look, but they're watching us."

"No surprise there." She sighed and started to lean back, but he held tightly onto her, keeping her close.

"They really are going to set you up with every eligible male on the island all winter, aren't they?"

"More like all year, but yes."

"So, let's give them what they want."

Her head dipped to the side. Maybe he was just as crazy as her mother. "I'm sorry, you've lost me. What?"

His eyes lit with amusement. "It's really quite simple. We pretend that we're dating." His gaze drifted in the direction of the two women intently watching them from the house. "If they think you are in a relationship, they won't keep thrusting unsuspecting men on you, and you won't have to pretend to not know what they're doing."

Part of her wanted to shout what a brilliant idea, the other part of her considered she might be as crazy as he was for even considering such an odd plan.

"They're still watching, aren't they?" His voice was low, and deep, and smooth as a top shelf whiskey.

She nodded.

"See what I mean? They're never going to give up. At least we can give you a pleasant and peaceful holiday season."

He did have a point. Though a bit out of the box, but then again, isn't that what SEALs were especially good at? Thinking outside the box. "How exactly do you see this going down?"

"We can go out now and again for a friendly meal or movie and whenever we're both at any of the family gatherings, we pretend we're actually together. You know, hold hands…"

Her gaze dropped to where his hand still covered hers.

"Maybe laugh together, sit together, and if they're watching, we could even stare into each others eyes like a couple of besotted teens."

That made her laugh. "Besotted, huh?"

"Smitten?" He shrugged.

"How old are you? Those are words my grandmother would have used."

"Mine too," he grinned at her, "which is probably why I use them. Grams was a firecracker."

From across the yard, when her mother and Maile should have been overseeing all the food and beverages for half the island, they were inside the patio doors, spying at them from behind the blinds. Kenny's idea, ridiculous as it was, had a silver lining. A holiday season free of her mother's scrutinizing gaze and Maile's not-so-subtle maneuvers. It was a tempting offer, a perfect solution to a problem she hadn't been able to solve on her own. He was offering her a shield, and she couldn't find a single reason to say no. "So, we keep holding hands, go to family dinners, and if you've got this right, I have the first ever Christmas season without having to look over my shoulder every five minutes, and then, after the new year, we can just say we make better friends than a couple?"

He nodded.

"And if it doesn't work?"

"No harm no foul."

"I suppose." Though she wasn't completely sure if this

was a brilliant idea or the worst one she'd ever heard.

"You know what we always say?"

Her gaze narrowed with his, not sure where he was going.

"Hope for the best, plan for the worst, and prepare to be surprised."

She chuckled at that, incredibly aware he was still holding her hand, and without looking knew her mother was still watching them. She just wasn't so sure she was ready for the worst—or any surprises—but she wouldn't mind the best. "Let's do it."

Kenny laughed, and Sara realized that for the first time in months, she wasn't dreading the rest of the holiday season. In fact, she was actually looking forward to it.

"So, boyfriend," she playfully tested out the word. "Tell me about your day."

"Well, girlfriend." Still smiling, Kenny settled back in his chair. "It just got a whole lot more interesting."

Of all the words that came to mind to describe this new bargain, she wasn't sure *interesting* was the one she'd have come up with, but it would do. "So, what do we do now?"

"Nothing." He shrugged. "If we lay it on too thick—"

"They'll never believe it." He was, of course, right. "In that case," she pushed to her feet, "I'd better go see what help is needed in the kitchen. Will I see you later?"

"Count on it."

And to her surprise, she was definitely looking forward to later.

The laughter and chatter of the party were a pleasant, low-level hum in Kenny's ears. Cutting through the maze of tables and people, he'd pause, smiling and chatting with friends and acquaintances. Every year the list of friends here on the island had grown considerably. Several of the men he'd once worked with like Nick, and Doug had settled on the island the Everett family called home.

Every so often he found himself glancing toward the house. From the yard, through the massive patio doors that extended across the living room and half the kitchen, he could see Sara elbow-deep in sudsy water, washing dishes alongside Emily and Angela while Maile directed traffic like a seasoned field commander, her voice cutting through the noise with clear, concise instructions that could be heard even from where he stood.

"You made up your mind yet?" Billy slapped him on the back. "There's always room for an experienced diver at the Big Island Dive Shop."

He knew that. For years, his friends had always made it clear he would be welcome, if not needed. Kenny had to admit, any time he'd gone with his friends on a group dive, he'd always enjoyed himself. More than he would have thought without a mission at stake.

"Now Billy, what did we agree?" Nick came up beside his longtime friend and business partner, shaking his head and rolling his eyes. "What part of the memo, give the man some time and space, did you not get?"

Kenny patted his friend on the arm. "No worries. We all know I have some decisions to make."

"Who knows," Billy shrugged. "Maybe you'll find a pirate's treasure and be set for life."

"What?" Kenny blinked.

"Don't mind him." Nick rolled his eyes. "We've had an unusual uptick in treasure hunters the last couple of years and it sometimes makes life a little crazy."

"Well, they do call Hawaii paradise," Billy reminded him, not for the first time. The mantra had been engrained in Billy's vocabulary since the first time Kenny had come to visit when everyone was still deployed together. "Angela has a friend from work she wants you to meet."

His head snapped around to face Billy. Was matchmaking genetic in the Everett family?

"Don't look so startled." Billy held back a laugh. "I told her you could find your own woman."

Bullet dodged. "Thanks." Kenny settled his hand on his buddy's shoulder. "I hate to eat and run, but it was a long flight yesterday and I've got a way to go before I catch up on the right time zone. I'm just going to thank your mom, and I'll see you guys tomorrow."

Everyone nodded and Kenny turned on his heel and marched to the kitchen. At first, he'd offered to fake date Sara just to keep the women from playing Dolly Levy on her, but it struck him that his offer was as good for him as it would be for her. He'd been on his fair share of blind dates thanks to the women in the Everrett family, some worse than others. This arrangement with Sara was going to ensure they both had a pleasant and unsupervised holiday.

Stepping past the open doors into the kitchen, he resisted the urge to wink at Sara when their eyes met briefly. This was a mission. He had a part to play. And a job to do—convince everyone that he and Sara were infatuated. "Maile, I can't thank you enough for another perfect evening. As always, the food was amazing, and the company even better."

His friend's mother gazed softly at him, her mouth tipped in a sweet smile. "You're leaving already?"

"Yes, ma'am. Long flight yesterday, and I'm still in the wrong time zone." Kenny grinned and turned toward Sara. "Sara, can I offer you a ride home?"

Sara looked up from the sink, suds clinging to her forearms. "Thanks, but I've got a ride with my parents."

Before Kenny could respond, Mrs. Alani appeared at his elbow as if summoned by magic. "Oh my," her voice pitched slightly higher than normal, "I promised to help Maile with…" She paused, her eyes wide open, a look of panicked realization on her face, her gaze darted from Sara to Maile, a silent SOS as she clearly scrambled for something plausible. "With…uh…"

Maile's eyes went wide for a split second before understanding dawned. "Oh yes, that's right, you did promise." She spun to face Sara, practically beaming. "You two run along. No sense making you wait around for your parents."

Kenny had to bite the inside of his cheek to keep from laughing. The two women were about as subtle as a freight train, but their enthusiasm was almost endearing.

"Are you sure, Mom?" Amusement danced in Sara's eyes.

"Absolutely sure." Mrs. Alani made shooing motions with her hands. "You go on. We'll be fine here."

"Well," Sara shrugged, untied her apron, and hung it on a nearby hook, "if you insist."

They made their way through the house and out to the front yard, maintaining their composure all the way to Kenny's rental car. Settling into their seats, Kenny caught sight of the two women peeking from behind the blinds.

"They're watching," Sara murmured.

"I see them." He backed out of the driveway slowly, resisting the urge to wave goodbye to their audience. They maintained their serious expressions until they reached the first stop sign, and then, as if someone had pulled the plug on a helium balloon, they both leaned forward, bursting with laughter.

"Who knew it would be so easy?" Sara gasped between giggles.

"And so much fun." Kenny shook his head in amazement. "Did you see your mother's face when she was trying to come up with an excuse?"

"I thought she was going to hyperventilate." Sara wiped tears from her eyes. "And Maile jumping in to save her was priceless."

"They're going to be planning our wedding by morning."

"Probably our children's names too."

Kenny turned onto the main road, still chuckling. To say the evening had taken an unexpected turn was the understatement of the decade. He glanced at the time on the dashboard. It was still early. "I'm not in a hurry to get home."

"Me either." The moonlight painted her profile in a soft, silver light.

"There's a great little place down by the water that serves incredible ice cream. What do you say to our first official fake-date?"

She looked at him, and her smile was real and unguarded. "I'm in."

CHAPTER SIX

Enjoying a comfortable, easy silence in the car, Sara leaned back in the seat. The stress of the evening, of knowing her mother and Maile were lurking behind every corner like a pair of benevolent but determined spies, had completely evaporated. It was an odd feeling, this sense of freedom, all thanks to a Navy SEAL and a ridiculously brilliant plan.

"I still can't believe how smoothly that went." She looked over at Kenny. The streetlights from the main road flashed across his face, illuminating the amused curve of his lips.

"Like a well-executed covert op." A hint of his military background showed in the simple response. "They never saw it coming."

Shaking her head, she chuckled. "I'm guessing they'd hoped and planned, but I think they were simply in shock that one of their efforts may have actually worked."

He glanced over at her, his smile widening. "It helps when your co-conspirator knows how to read the room."

"I'll take that as a compliment."

"As it was intended."

Her gaze on the road ahead, she relaxed into the easy rhythm of the car. The lack of pressure to be the perfect conversationalist, the perfect companion, the perfect...everything, was oddly refreshing. No need for nervous chatter, no waiting out awkward silences. They were simply two people in on a joke, and it was a really good joke.

Turning off the main road, he followed a narrow lane and pulled into a small, brightly lit parking lot. "This is the place I was telling you about."

A small, wooden building sat nestled between a couple of surf shops, its windows glowing with a warm, inviting light, sported a massive hand painted sign, Woody's.

"Great choice. Woody's is known for their hand churned ice cream. They don't have many flavors, but what they do have is fabulous."

"And here I thought I'd discovered an island secret," he teased good naturedly as they stepped out of the car.

The evening air infused with the sweet scent of waffle cones had already summoned a small crowd. A line had formed outside, people laughing and talking, clearly enjoying the cool night. Taking their place in line, they fell into a comfortable rhythm, their shoulders brushing from time to time as they moved forward. Once they got close enough to see the handwritten chalkboard with the regular flavors and the day's specials, Sara observed the way his eyes scanned the menu with a focused concentration that seemed a bit over-the-top for ice cream flavors. She'd seen that same look in her other former Navy friends. Whether this intensity was what drew them to be Navy SEALs and divers, or the Navy was what taught them to treat every incident no matter how big or small with the focus of a life or death situation, she had no idea. Either way, she was sure that he was a man who planned his approach, whether it was to a hostile environment or a dessert counter. Considering the carefree, almost careless behavior of most of the men she'd known or dated, especially freeloading Vinny, she rather appreciated the man she was getting to know.

"Know what you'd like?"

She bobbed her head. With only six flavors to choose from, her decision was easy. "I'm a creature of habit. Coconut macadamia." She pointed to the tropical-looking scoop in the case. "It's been my go-to since I was twelve."

"Can't argue with tradition." Kenny grinned and turned to the teenager behind the counter. "We'll each have two scoops of the coconut macadamia."

They took their waffle cones and found an empty table outside the shop. Settling in across from her, his long legs stretched out under the table. She licked a bit of melted ice cream from the side of her cone. When she lifted her gaze, she caught him watching her, a ghost of a smile on his face. She had to admit, this felt surprisingly normal. Not awkward or forced like she'd expected from a fake dating arrangement, but genuinely pleasant.

Kenny twirled his cone, licking the melting drips. "I really love their ice cream."

"Me too." There didn't seem to be a need to say anything more, to fill the silence with empty words. She liked that. She licked at her ice cream, savoring the treat, and when the risk of melting all over her hand was gone, she glanced up at him. "Tell me something."

Kenny nodded.

"What does a Navy SEAL do for fun?"

"Honestly?" He licked at a drip running down his cone before leveling his gaze with hers. "For the last twenty years, whatever the Navy told me to do. I'm still figuring out what to do now for myself. It feels a little odd not knowing what I'm supposed to do next."

"Well, if it makes you feel any better, I never had the Navy telling me what to do and I'm still trying to figure what I want from life—besides a home of my own." She paused a moment. "Though, I suppose, some might say along the way I spent twenty years doing what my mother told me."

"Then I guess we have something in common." Kenny laughed, and Sara realized she liked the sound. "What do you think they're doing right now? Your mother and Maile."

"Probably calling everyone they know to share the good news that Sara finally has a boyfriend who isn't a bum." Sara shook her head. "My money's on Mom's already planning what she's going to wear to our wedding."

"You think?" He paused mid-lick, thick dark brows buckling over surprisingly deep blue eyes.

"Are you kidding?" Sara bit back a laugh. "They've been trying to match me up with anyone for so long that they have to be thinking their brilliant matchmaking finally worked."

He nibbled at the corner of his cone, and she tried not to stare. "We just gave them exactly what they wanted to see."

"Exactly." She went back to licking her ice cream.

"In other words," he smiled at her, "mission accomplished."

She nodded and when their cones were finished, she pushed to her feet, Kenny following. Each tossed their napkins and empty cups into the trash and strolled away. The night was warm and pleasant, with just enough breeze to remind them this was paradise.

"Would you like to take a short walk down to the beach?" He nodded toward the path that led to the water. "Unless you're too tired."

"Not tired at all." Fake dating was so much more fun than real dating that she'd actually been trying to think of a way to extend their time together. "Lead the way."

The sound of waves hitting the shore never got old. Kenny had walked beaches on various continents, but there was something about Hawaiian sand between his toes that felt more like he belonged here than any other beach. Maybe it was all the years of visiting Billy and the Everrett family, or maybe it was just the way the moonlight turned the water silver.

"You're quiet," Sara said, walking beside him with her sandals dangling from her fingers.

"Just thinking." Kenny inhaled the salt air, feeling his shoulders relax in a way they hadn't in months. "I've always known these are the best beaches, but somehow my mind always forgets just how peaceful this place is."

"Different from your usual work environment, I'm guessing."

"You could say that." Watching her, he couldn't help but notice how the moonlight caught the red highlights in her hair. He bent down, picking up a small, perfectly spiral shell that was half-buried in the sand. He held it out to her, the delicate curves of its interior gleaming in the evening light. "You can tell the tides are high. This one's still damp."

Sara took the shell, turning it over in her palm. "You can tell that just from looking at this shell?"

"That and the way the waves are coming in. They're higher on the beach than the dry line." He gestured with his free hand to a darker strip of sand near the water's edge. "And the fact that the shell has that perfect sheen of moisture on it."

"You're really good at this. Noticing the small things."

"It's a requirement of the job." He shrugged, keeping his tone light. "In my line of work, the small things can mean the difference between a good day and a bad one. A misplaced pebble, a snapped twig. You learn to absorb everything."

"Like what?"

Kenny thought for a moment. "The color of someone's shoes, the way they hold their coffee cup, whether they're right or left-handed. The layout of a room, who sat where, what they ordered for lunch three weeks ago." He picked up another piece of driftwood. "It becomes automatic after a while."

"That's actually pretty impressive."

"It has its downsides. I remember everything. Including things I'd rather forget."

"I can't imagine facing situations that every minute could be the difference between life and death. It must be hard."

"Not for me. It's how I'm wired. It doesn't hurt that I've always had a near photographic memory. As a kid in school, if I didn't remember the answer to a question on a test, I'd close my eyes and scan my notes in my mind and find the answer."

"Dang. Wish I could have done that." She snorted more than laughed. "Heck, I'd kill to be able to do that now. Half the time I forget where I put my car keys or if my favorite blouse is clean or dirty."

He chuckled softly. "Yeah, well, I have those moments

too. Just not when I'm working."

Sara was quiet for a moment, and Kenny wondered if he'd said too much. But then she smiled. "I bet you remember the song playing the first time you charmed a girl into the back seat of your car."

"Stairway to Heaven."

"You're kidding."

Holding back a grin, he waved his hands palm up. "Hey, you asked."

Sara burst out laughing. "Please tell me you didn't actually sing along."

"I'm not admitting anything without a lawyer present."

Still chuckling softly, her head bobbed and her gaze remained on the beach ahead. They walked in comfortable silence for a few minutes, when her steps slowed. "What's your favorite movie?"

"*The Hunt for Red October.*"

"Of course it is." Her grin widened. "Very military of you."

"What can I say? I like submarines and Sean Connery." Kenny found himself studying her profile as they walked. "What's yours?"

"*My Cousin Vinny.* No matter how many times I've seen the movie, it always makes me laugh."

"Me too. Great film. Maybe we can watch it on our next fake date."

"Sounds good." She nodded. "Do you have a favorite color?"

"Blue. Not sure if I've always liked the color because I've always been drawn to the ocean, or if I was drawn to the ocean because I loved the color blue."

"A little like the chicken or the egg."

He chuckled. "Something like that." Smiling, he turned his head to face her. "Your favorite color is green."

She stopped short. "Did I tell you that?"

"No." He shook his head. "Every time I've seen you, you're always in a green dress. And if you're not, you're accessorizing with green."

"Then I don't need to tell you that I have a green accent

wall in my bedroom."

There was no way he was going to let himself start imagining her bedroom. "Your favorite song?"

"You don't know already?"

How is it this woman had a way of making him smile so much his cheeks were actually hurting. "You've never played any music while I was around."

"Fair enough." They took a few more steps, but she didn't say a word.

"And…?"

"What?"

"Your favorite song? Are you going to tell me?"

A cheeky grin on her face, she beamed up at him. "I haven't decided. A woman is entitled to some mystery."

"You are something else." He laughed harder than he had all night. Something told him, fake dating or not, the rest of the holidays were definitely going to be like none other. "What's your schedule tomorrow?"

She shook her head. "I'm off work."

"Good." He slowed his stride as they drew closer to where he'd parked the car. "Let's say I pick you up at noon."

"Noon?"

"For our second *first* date. Will your mom be home then?"

She nodded, her eyes shifting from confusion to sparkling with understanding. "She will. Where are we going to go?"

"Ah." He dared to reach over and swipe down her nose with his finger. "I can be a man of mystery too."

When she burst out laughing rather then slug him for his cheekiness, he decided he might actually enjoy this little charade of theirs. Maybe a lot.

CHAPTER SEVEN

Normally, Sara loved to sleep in on a day off. Not till an insane time of day, but at least not rising with the sun like she did on a work day. No matter how many times she tossed, turned, or fluffed her pillow, sleeping in was not going to happen.

After staring at the contents of her closet for close to half an hour, she finally gave up on deciding what would be appropriate and texted Kenny. *What should I wear?*

Sitting on the edge of her bed, she stared at the screen. This shouldn't be such a big deal. A sundress would be good for anything on the island. Or maybe a pair of shorts and a comfortable top? Then if he had some warped SEAL sense of humor and wanted to take her on mountain hike or some other endurance trek, she wouldn't be worried about flashing the world in a skirt.

Her phone dinged and she almost jumped up from the bed. *Anything you like. And comfortable shoes.*

Comfortable shoes? So maybe the big bad SEAL really was going to take her to an obstacle course suitable for Coronado? Swinging the closet doors open again, she opted for practical. No one wears a sundress with comfortable shoes. She pulled out her favorite green capris and paired it with a three quarter sleeve, boat neck cream colored cotton top. Her slip on canvas loafers with rubber soles definitely qualified as comfortable—and practical if she actually did wind up doing an obstacle course.

Glancing in the mirror, she looked pretty darn good if she did say so herself. What she didn't understand was why was she so nervous over fake date number two? Maybe it was muscle memory. A man asks you out—a handsome one at that—and it's a knee jerk reaction to fret. She was not going to do that anymore. No matter what they were making her parents and Maile Everrett think, she and Kenny were just friends. New found friends, but definitely only friends.

The doorbell rang and her heart lurched to her throat. "Just friends," she gently reminded herself before stopping herself from galloping down the stairs. Taking a deep breath, reminding herself one more time that this wasn't a real date, she swung the door open. Kenny was hidden behind a massive bouquet of multicolored blooms. One of the largest she'd ever seen not in a vase, and certainly the biggest she'd ever been given. Not that she'd been given flowers all that often.

"Too much?" He held them out and smiled.

Was it her imagination or was Mr. Confident SEAL nervous. "They're perfect." She took a deep whiff. The scent was heavenly. "Thank you."

"Who is it, dear?"

As if her mother didn't know. The woman had probably been peering out the window the moment she heard the car pull up to the curb.

"Why, Kenny. What a surprise."

It took everything in Sara not to roll her eyes. This was, after all, what they'd wanted, her mother to believe her daughter had finally hooked a man. Now all she had to do was reel him in.

"It's nice to see you Mrs. Alani."

"Please, call me Missy."

"Yes, ma'am." Kenny's gaze darted from her mother to Sara, his smile instantly spreading so wide and sincere that her knees actually wobbled. Lord, could this man act. Probably something he'd had to do more than once as a SEAL when the stakes were much higher than what two mothers believed. "You look lovely."

From the heat in her cheeks she knew she had to be blushing a hundred shades of red. "Thank you. I'll put these in water and then we can go."

"No need." Her mom took the flowers from her hands. "I'll take care of it. You two run along and have a nice afternoon." Only a few steps away, her mom paused. "Should I pack you something to eat?"

"No, ma'am. We're all set."

Her mother shook her head. "I guess Missy will take some practice." Without waiting for his response, she turned on her heel and scurried into the kitchen.

"You really do look beautiful," his voice was low, and deep, and soothing as honey to a sore throat.

"Thank you."

Extending his elbow to her, he gestured toward his car. At the curb, he opened the passenger door, waited for her to be seated, and then circled the hood, taking his place behind the wheel. "I hope you like picnics."

"Love them. Ants not so much, but picnics can be lots of fun."

"Good."

"What would you have done if I'd said no?"

"Plan B."

Her head tipped and she studied him for a second wondering if he really would have changed his plans, and then she remembered. "Plan for the best, prepare for the worst, and expect to be surprised."

"That's my girl."

My girl? He did know he didn't have to play the part with her, didn't he?

"We're not going far. Another fifteen or twenty minutes tops."

She shrugged. "This is Kona, nothing is very far."

"Good point."

He hit the blinker arm and turned left up a street that Sara had never been on. Her mind quickly running through all the parks and picnic spots she knew of that weren't on a beach. She was drawing a blank. "How'd you sleep?"

"Like a baby. That hotel has some seriously comfortable beds. The first night was a bit jarring. Every time I rolled over, expecting the firmness of a cot mattress beneath me, I was jolted awake at the softness of a cloud."

"But not last night?"

He shook his head. "With each night, I was less

surprised, and by last night, a bomb couldn't have woken me."

Too bad she couldn't say the same.

For the next few minutes they discussed everything from the food at the hotel to her mother's reaction to the flowers. When he turned off the street onto a nearly dirt road, she forgot to carry her end of the conversation, focusing on all the shrubs and trees, and overgrown land around them. "Where are we going?"

"You'll see. We're almost there." Once they came around a wide curve, he pulled down another dirt road that bounced them all the way to a clearing at the edge of the hill. Unlike the rest of the surrounding wild landscape, this patch of land was grassy, freshly mowed, and had a single unpainted picnic table dead center. Thank heaven. Just as he'd done when she entered the car, he trotted around the hood and opened her door. "Where the creature comforts are lacking, the view should make up for it."

By the time they reached the table, the shore below was in plain sight. Her jaw dropped ever so slightly and those beautiful green eyes circled round. "Wow."

"That's what I thought."

"How did you find this place?" She glanced around one hundred and eighty degrees. "Should we even be here?"

"First, I found this place about ten years ago when I was on leave visiting Billy. I got bored and went for a drive. Did a little exploring."

Her head turning to the hillside across the dirt road that reminded him, and probably everyone else, of a jungle movie. Her gaze leveled with his. "Did you bring your machete?"

Setting down the picnic basket he'd grabbed from the trunk, he burst out laughing. "Almost. But not quite."

She sniffed at the air, clearly distracted by the aromas of fried chicken and fresh rolls.

"Another perk of a luxury resort. They know how to put a picnic lunch together." He pulled out several containers, napkins, plastic plates and silverware.

"The Kings Hotel knows how to do a lot."

"No argument there."

"So why is this the only mowed lot? And why is there a picnic table here?"

"I called to have it cleared before I left my last post, and ordered the table delivered this morning."

"What?"

He chuckled softly. "Maybe I should backtrack. When I came wandering up here all those years ago, there was a For Sale sign down the hill. The owner didn't trust realtors and not a whole lot of people like trekking through a near jungle for fun."

"I guess not everyone on this island were SEALs."

"Probably not. Anyhow, this hillside had been in the family for generations. But the owner had one problem."

"Only one?"

He stifled the urge to roll his eyes at her teasing. "Let's say only one that I knew of. He was the last in his family. No wife. No kids. No one to inherit."

"Oh." She slid onto the bench. "That's sad. Everyone should have a legacy of some kind."

"That's what I thought. Which is why I bought it."

"You bought the lot?"

He shook his head. "I bought the whole mountainside."

If it were possible for a woman's eyes to fall out of her head, Sara's looked like they just might.

"Lemonade or wine?"

She blinked. "Lemonade. I have a feeling I'm going to need full mastery of my wits today."

This woman not only had an endearing sense of humor, she rolled with the punches better than any woman he'd ever dated. Not that they were dating, and not that his career had allowed much time for anything close to a long-term relationship. What he didn't understand was why the heck some smart man hadn't snapped her up a long time ago.

"Lemonade it is."

Still looking around, she barely shook her head before blowing out a low sigh. "Did you really buy all this?"

"I did." He nodded.

"I had no clue SEALs made that much money. Or are you independently wealthy and no one ever mentioned it? Because if you are, my mother may never let you get away."

"Not independently wealthy. We don't make that much money, though we made a nice living. We did get paid some nice bonuses though, lots of overseas assignments come with hazard pay."

"Like engineers in the Middle East."

He nodded. "The military paid a lot of money to train us, and like fighter pilots, they don't want to lose us. What helped is that my expenses when deployed for months on end were minimal so my savings grew exponentially." He shrugged. "With a little investment help."

Again, she looked around shaking her head. "You're going to have to show me about that investment part."

"Not being risk averse helps. Took a few chances that tanked, took a few others that soared. It also didn't hurt that the owner liked me, had no other offers, wanted to leave the island and move stateside with some old Navy buddies. Some place in Central Florida. Lots of houses, planned activities and once upon a time, an STD ratio that made you think twice about what it meant to grow old gracefully."

"You're kidding?" The wide eyes were gone and now sparkling with humor.

"Nope. Dead serious."

She reached for a piece of chicken. "You said you didn't know what you were going to do next. If you were going to stay or move on."

"That's right." He scooped some potato salad on his plate and offered her some.

"Just a little." She handed him a napkin and plastic silverware. "If you leave, what will you do with all this land?"

And that had been just one of the many questions he'd been asking himself since the day he put in his papers.

"What would you do with it? If it were yours?"

Her gaze drifted to the distant ocean views. "Hmm, that's tough. It's so open here. I suppose I'd plant a nice big tree in the front yard and another in the back, just to make things seem homey, and shady."

Intrigued by her perspective, he nodded.

"You'd want all the main rooms to have a view the ocean, so things that don't matter like garages, laundry rooms, bathrooms and pantries would face the front of the home, and anyplace you'd hang out you would be able to enjoy the views."

Interesting that she'd called it a home, not a house. Turning to look at the view she was staring at as if she could see the house coming together in front of her, he had to admit she had a good point about focusing on the views.

"I'd keep the interior spacious, not clutter it with too much but still have soft fabrics and colors to bring in the warmth and make it feel like a home not a magazine shoot."

As she continued to run through her vision for the house, he could almost see it coming together. Too bad, even with a home design in mind, he had no idea what to do with the rest of his life.

CHAPTER EIGHT

"The question now, is do we do something else? Or do I take you home and hope that a picnic lunch is enough to satiate your mother's matchmaking urges?" Kenny had planned for something else this afternoon, but didn't want to assume.

Wiping the corners of her mouth with a paper napkin, Sara looked out over the ocean view and then looked back at him. "I suppose coming home right away might give her the idea that things didn't go well."

Relief washed over him. He hadn't realized until this very second how much he didn't want the day to end. "Then it's back to the hotel."

Her eyes flew open wide and he realized that didn't come out the way he'd meant.

"They have an afternoon scavenger hunt. I thought it could be fun. First prize is a dinner at the rooftop restaurant."

"I've seen folks running all over the hotel like a bunch of teenagers on prom night."

"Have you ever participated?"

She shook her head. "Nope. The hunt is only for guests."

"Will participating with me pose any problems for your job?"

Tipping her head to one side, she stared at him as if the solution to world peace was engraved on his forehead. "Working here might be seen as giving me an unfair advantage, but I really don't spend much time on the main grounds only the rooms, so, I think it will be all right."

"Do you want to do it?"

Her head still tilted slightly, a sweet smile bloomed at the edges of her lips. "Might be fun."

"Then a scavenger hunt it is." He pushed to his feet, gathering up the leftovers from their lunch.

Sara reached over, bagging all the trash. "I'm going to guess, because of your job and that keen memory of yours, you're probably pretty good at this sort of thing."

He shrugged. "Maybe."

The five star resort lobby hummed with quiet elegance. A trio of musicians played easy listening tunes recognizable by anyone over the age of forty, their sound floating through the soaring open space. Guests lingered in linen and sundresses, laughter muted as everyone instinctively matched the tone of the grand hotel.

Kenny glanced at Sara beside him, her smile uncertain but curious. "Ready to do this?"

Taking in a deep breath, she bobbed her head.

At a nearby table, a framed poster announcing the afternoon scavenger hunt rested on an antique brass easel. Beside it, a polished young attendant handed over a printed sheet. "Here you are, sir. The hunt begins in twenty minutes. Teams have two hours to photograph and check off each item on the list. The first group to return with all the items found wins a dinner at our rooftop restaurant."

While he hadn't dined at the famed restaurant, he knew from his evening at the bar that this prize was worth winning. Especially for another fake date with Sara. Kenny accepted the paper, thanked the man, then moved aside. He skimmed the first challenge and had to bite back a grin. "Find the oil painting with seven palm trees."

Sara's brow arched. "You already know, don't you?"

"Maybe." He couldn't help it—he liked watching her exasperation turn into amusement.

Together, they studied the list for the next several minutes until the gentleman by the table announced to the people scattered about that the hunt would begin in two minutes. He already remembered where a handful of the unusual items might be. For instance, he noticed his first day at the hotel that between the lobby and the pool, the hallway was lined with pastoral scenes. From the first to the last painting the number of palm trees grew from one lone tree at the first location to a full-fledged grove by the last painting. It had taken a moment, but then he realized each painting had one more palm.

The woman at the table gently clapped her hands together, calling all the participants to her. Once again she explained the rules, the timeframe, and of course, pimped all the delicious foods at their prized restaurant. His mouth almost watered from the brief description she'd given.

He led her through the glass doors, the soft trickle of water greeting them as the sunlight caught polished stone. Without hesitation, walking in a quick clip, counting. "One, two, three, four, five, six, and seven." At the last painting on the wall, he stopped and waved a thumb over his shoulder. "Check off the seven palms."

Sara leaned forward, her eyes darting about, counting palm trees. She straightened to her full height, then turned to face him. "How did you do that?"

He shrugged. "I notice patterns. This is seven of eight paintings. They each have one more palm than the one before."

Taking a step back and glancing down the wall, he watched as she counted each palm tree in multiple paintings before shaking her head and softly chuckling. "Show-off."

"Just observant." He caught the faintest flush on her cheeks, then glanced back at the list. "Next one—find the wooden carving of a turtle."

For a quick moment, he closed his eyes and as if his mind were an old fashioned Rolodex, flipped the images one after another until he stopped at the turtle. "Follow me."

They returned to the lobby, her soft soled shoes barely tapping against the sleek marble flooring. Kenny didn't even slow down as he stopped at the staircase, pulling out his phone and snapping a shot of a two foot turtle resting under one corner of the staircase, a star fish, an octopus, and a jelly fish deliberately hung from string under the same steps, creating a wooden seaside landscape.

"You remembered this?"

He nodded. "For what it's worth, there's another display like this near the tennis courts with flamingos, seagulls, and a peacock."

"How many flamingos?"

Holding back a smile, he blinked. "Four."

Her head bobbed. "I seriously wish you'd sat next to me in Chemistry."

Without thinking, he burst out laughing. "I wasn't quite as observant in high school." No need to mention in those days, his life didn't depend on his observation skills.

The next clue read: "Locate the historic photograph from the hotel's opening."

"Ooh." She nearly danced in place. "I know this one." Grabbing his hand she bolted across the lobby, forcing him to widen his stride to keep up with her pace. Circling around the massive Christmas tree in the center of the massive lobby, she continued across the hotel, stopping just inside the pool doorway, she straightened, proudly pointing. "There it is."

Quickly, he snapped a photo. "We make a good team." Judging by her smile, he guessed she agreed.

Who knew running around a hotel with a Navy SEAL could be some of the most fun she'd had in years. And when she said running, she was not exaggerating. This man could move. Besides a keen sense of observation and an astounding memory, he'd taken hold of her hand to lead her out onto the lanai and down the shore to the beach chair shack to photograph the cluster of blue crabs on the shack wall, and had yet to let go. More important, she was glad.

They'd worked their way through most of the list with military efficiency. Kenny seemed to have a mental map of the entire resort, locating items with the kind of precision that made Sara wonder what else that brain of his stored away. Next on the list: Find the blue Christmas tree.

"Blue?" Kenny frowned.

Sara nodded. "Every tree in the hotel, and there are a lot of them, all of them have different themes. Sometimes it's scenic, like Santa and his workshop, or everything beachy, but there's always colors too." Her cheeks tugged at the corners of her mouth. "And as it just so happens, I know where the blue tree is." Hurrying back across the lobby again, she stopped at the entrance to the ladies room. "Hand me your phone."

Nodding, he extended his hand, a sparkling smile taking over his face.

In another minute she'd photographed the tree and handing him back his phone, leaned against him to read the list. Shoulders pressing, she momentarily forgot why she was standing so close. The man had arms like steel.

"They've definitely shifted into the holiday mood. Santa's favorite helper." His brows pleated and deep lines formed between his brows. "I don't remember seeing anything with elves. Or anything that looks like elves."

He had her there. She didn't know of anything with elves at all. Except for when the season was in full swing, then the Santa's Village had human elves, but they weren't set up yet.

"I'm stumped." Kenny shook his head.

"What if it's not an elf?"

His brows shot up. "Then who?" His eyes darted left and right, then up and down as if doing an eye exam. Lifting his hand, he snapped his fingers. "Mrs. Claus?"

It came out more like a question, but it was the hint she needed. "Of course."

Scurrying behind her, despite his height, he actually had to scramble to catch up. "Of course what?"

"Santa's Village." She pointed ahead to an area behind the pool. "They take half the tennis courts and set up a Santa's village every year. It's almost ready."

"I haven't been to this part of the resort."

"Of course you haven't. Otherwise, you'd remember this." Pleased with herself, she pointed to the sign announcing the impending arrival of the village. A life size Mrs. Claus happily smiling at the guests.

"You, Miss Alani, are a genius."

"I don't know about that, but there's a lot to be said for this teamwork thing."

They practically jogged back to the activities table. The young attendant's eyes widened as she reviewed their photos and checklist. "Congratulations! Not only are you our winners, but you've set a new record for completion time." She promptly handed over an embossed envelope. "This will be valid any time in the next thirty days."

"Thank you." Their two voices tumbled over each other.

Kenny tucked the prize into his pocket, then gestured toward the front doorway. "So, when do you want to do this lovely dinner?"

Right now rushed to mind. Not too pushy. "Any night off will be great."

His head bobbed once and reaching his car, he opened the door for her. "Would tonight be too soon?"

"Tonight?" Had he read her mind?

"We can wait if you'd prefer?"

"No," she shook her head, "tonight would be great. I don't always know when I'm going to get a night off, or pick up extra shifts."

"Great." He closed the door and circled the hood, taking his seat on the driver's side. "I'll drop you off, come back to shower and change, and call for reservations."

"Perfect. Just let me know what time you'll be picking me up."

On the drive home, the sun still shone in the sky. Bright, warm, and a happy yellow. In an odd way, at this moment, she felt as happy as the sun. "Thank you. That was way more fun than I expected."

"It was, wasn't it?" His lips curled in the slightest of smiles.

When he pulled up to her parents' house, she spotted the curtains twitch. "And here we go."

Kenny's gaze followed hers, and with that keen eye for observation, he no doubt saw what she'd seen. "Showtime."

Right. Showtime. She'd almost forgotten, this was

nothing more than a performance for the matchmaking mothers.

Kenny got out and walked around to open her door, ever the gentleman. As they approached her front door, Sara was acutely aware that they were still holding hands. "Thank you again for today." She turned to face him on the porch. "All of it was the most fun I've had in a long time."

"We'll have to work on that then, but for the record, me too."

For a moment they stood there, looking at each other, and Sara realized Kenny was thinking the same thing she was. Simply holding hands to the door wouldn't be enough for the pretense.

"We should probably…" Kenny's voice trailed off as his gaze flicked toward the front window.

"Give them something to talk about?" Sara finished.

"Something like that, yeah." Kenny's voice was low and deep and barely audible. His hand came up to cup her cheek. His eyes searched hers for a moment before he leaned in slowly, giving her plenty of time to pull away if she wanted.

She didn't want to. His lips were warm and gentle, and the kiss lasted just long enough to look real without crossing any lines.

"See you tonight." He inched back slowly.

"Tonight." She nodded.

In a ridiculous effort to extend the moment, instead of going inside, she watched Kenny walk to his car. Not wanting to look foolish, standing there until he drove away, she turned and let herself into the house. She almost laughed at her mother trying very hard to look like she'd been dusting and not spying from the living room window. Considering her mother only dusted when company was coming, the woman was pretty much busted. Straightening her shoulders, sucking in a fortifying breath, Sara repeated what Kenny had said in the car: *Showtime.*

CHAPTER NINE

"He kissed her? So soon?" Maile Everrett's voice rang clear in Missy's ear.

"Not a big kiss. Just a..." she searched for the right word, "sweet kiss."

"Hmm," her dearest friend of decades huffed. "I expected more from our Kenny."

Shaking her head even though her friend couldn't see, Missy sighed. "He opened the car door for her."

"Good. Good," Maile muttered.

"When she was out of the car he didn't let go of her hand."

"Wait. He held her hand?"

"That's right. He extended it to help her out of the car and once they were on the curb, he didn't let go."

"I see." The tone in Maile's voice had softened. "And he walked her to the door?"

"Yes."

"Maybe there's hope for our Kenny."

She didn't say it out loud, but Missy raised her gaze to the ceiling of her bedroom closet, the only place no one in the house could hear her talking on the phone, and prayed today meant there was hope for her Sara. Her little girl with the most tender heart deserved a man as good as her father. With the grace of God, maybe, just maybe this time, everything would work out.

By the time Kenny pulled up in front of the house again,

twilight had settled in. The last of the sun's glow streaked the horizon, and the streetlights shone on the roads below. Before he could make it halfway down the front path, Sara stepped out the front door. For a split second Kenny almost forgot this wasn't a real date. Extending his elbow to her, he caught the faintest movement of the curtains again. "Maybe I should have kissed you hello?"

Her eyes rolled heavenward. "Do I need to ask if they're watching?"

"You know they are."

"Yeah," she sighed, "I do. And no. Leading the way is more chivalrous in their minds. I suspect you've scored a few brownie points."

"Got it." He smiled, holding the car door open for her. Quickly circling the hood, he climbed into the driver seat and was still grinning when he pulled away from the curb. This was definitely proving to be a very different way of spending his holiday. "How did it go earlier?"

"To my surprise, no third degree. Though I will say, it was rather entertaining watching Mom pretend to dust every surface in the living room so I wouldn't know she'd been spying from the window. It must have killed her not to ask me a thousand questions, but I could see her eyes brighten when I told her I was home to change for dinner tonight."

The Alani's didn't live far from the resort. Honestly, even though it was the Big Island, getting to the other side of the island was no more than the time it might take to get through rush hour traffic in a big city. "I was able to secure a reservation for a table by a window."

Her brows rose high over her wide eyes. "What did you do? Slip the maitre d your life savings?"

"Not exactly." He turned into the resort parking lot. "But when I stopped by on my way out of the resort to make my request, the young man at the podium noted my haircut. He asked if I was on leave from Pearl Harbor. I explained I'd already done my twenty and was joining the ranks of a civilian. One question led to another and when I mentioned I'd been a SEAL, next thing I knew, there was a reserved sign on the best table in the place."

"Ah, he has a thing for SEALs?"

Kenny shook his head. "Not exactly. Seems his grandfather was a SEAL. Told me the man would fly back from the main land to kick his butt if he didn't treat me right."

"Well, good for Grandpa."

That was pretty much what he thought. Even if all of this was free and just for show, deep down, he wanted her to have a really nice time. To be treated the way she deserved.

"Have you eaten here before?" He pushed the button to the top floor dining room.

"Nope." She shook her head. "Only seen a glimpse in passing on my way to bathroom duty. And I don't do that very often."

The elevator dinged, and placing his hand on the small of her back, he ushered her out of the small space and across the expansive hall to the large double glass doors that led to the five star restaurant.

"Oh, my."

Even he blinked. When he'd been there a short time ago he'd noticed that the place was fully decked out for upcoming holidays, but it had not been nearly as impactful as it was at this moment. A breathtaking expanse of festive elegance, the restaurant was worthy of a state dinner. In the corner, a magnificent, Christmas tree stood almost touching the high ceilings, its boughs shimmering with strands of multi colored lights reflecting off the shiny ornaments in every shape imaginable. Strategically placed bows in golds and reds added to the wow factor. "Definitely beginning to feel a lot like Christmas."

"Every year I think the resort can't outdo last year, and every year they surprise me." Her gaze darted from one table to the next taking in the variety of themed centerpieces. Some had tea lights of green, white, and red in stemmed glassware of different heights, others had arrangements of red and white flowers perched on a gold rimmed glass vase with a crystal teardrop hanging within. Each table was as impressive as the one before.

The host, a different gentleman, greeted them. "Good

evening. Welcome to the Plumeria. Do you have a reservation?"

"For two. Yates."

"Ah, yes, Mr. Yates. Follow me."

Their table was tucked in a private corner with stunning views through the plate glass windows of the dark sea below and equally sparkling views of the tree across the way. They'd barely settled into their seats when the small band across the way began to play. It took a minute for him to recognize the tune.

"Oh, I love this song." Her face lit up as bright as the Christmas tree. "Actually, I pretty much like anything Michael Buble sings."

He shrugged. "He's okay, but there's no one like the original crooner... Sinatra."

"Now I know my mom would love you. Sinatra is her favorite."

"So your mom has good taste."

Sara chuckled softly, reaching for her napkin.

Kenny pushed to his feet and stretched his hand out in front of her. "Can't let a good song go to waste, even if it's not a Sinatra tune. Join me?"

Sara looked at Kenny's outstretched hand, then at the small dance floor where a few other couples swayed to the music. "You are a risk taker, aren't you?"

"It's in my DNA." The smile that teased his lips had her toes tingling.

Sara placed her hand in his and Kenny led her to the dance floor. One hand settling at her waist while the other held hers gently, they moved slowly to Michael Bublé's smooth voice. "You didn't warn me you're a good dancer."

"Not that good."

"Better than me."

"I don't know about that." Gently, he raised her one arm high, spun her out then pulled her back in, pulling her flawlessly against him without letting her miss a single step.

"I feel like Ginger Rogers. I can't believe I did that move and didn't trip over my own two feet."

If that wasn't enough, the song picked up speed and pulling her closer, his grip tightening around her waist, he slipped his foot between her feet and leaning right, spun them around the dance floor like a twirling figurine atop a music box. They came to a stop at the same time the music slowed to the end. "You're better than Ginger."

Her hand on her chest, she stood perfectly still, staring up at her fake date. "No one is going to believe I did that."

The corner of his mouth lifted, more amused than smug. "It could be our little secret?"

Now why did the idea of keeping secrets with Navy SEAL Kenny Yates hold so much appeal?

"Or," his brows rose a little higher, "we could show off for your family."

"Yeah, no. That might be a bit of overkill."

A softer tune kicked in and Kenny continued to hold her close as they glided around the dance floor. "So what's next? Do you have any more days off?"

"I'm working the day shift this week. I get off work around three pm usually. So far, no opportunities to pick up extra night shifts have come my way."

"So, I hear that downtown is getting all decked out for the season."

She nodded.

"I'm told there's a fun parade."

"That's right. It starts the season." As a kid the inaugural parade to kick off the holidays was always one of her favorite things to do.

"I usually start my Christmas shopping much earlier than this, but this year has been a little unusual. Would you care to join me after work? Help me do a little shopping, then watch the parade."

She couldn't resist the smile that tugged at the corners of her mouth. She hadn't been able to attend the parade in years. "I think I'd like that."

"Good. Then it's a date."

A date. Oh, in only a few days, that word was starting to take on a whole new meaning for her. She sure hoped she hadn't gotten in over her head.

Dining and dancing with Sara had been the nicest evening he could remember having in a heck of a long time. He hadn't expected to have a bad time, but Kenny hadn't expected to enjoy her company near as much as he was. Not only was she an easy dance partner, following his lead with the lightest of nudges, she laughed at all his jokes—and not a forced polite laugh, but an honest and appreciative reaction. And her eyes didn't glaze over when he'd forget himself and talked a little too much about life in Uncle Sam's Navy…at least what he was free to share.

"Hey, isn't this a surprise." Holding hands with his wife, Nick Harper came up behind him.

"Hey there." Kenny pushed to his feet. Some things the Navy drilled into a sailor for life. Right along side of never put your hands in your pockets or wear your cover indoors, there was also the rule to always stand for a lady or superior officer. Too bad he had to ignore the code of never lie to a buddy. "Celebrating something?"

"My mother is in town and babysitting. That's reason enough," Nick teased.

"We're just about to order dessert. Care to join us?" Kenny waved at the two empty chairs on either side of him.

Nick shook his head. "Nope. Have to call it an early night. I've got a lot of prep work to do for a new group of amateur treasure hunters renting one of our boats for the next couple of weeks."

"Treasure hunters?" Kenny's one brow rose up.

"Yeah," Nick sighed. "Some of these folks are great, and some are reckless as hell. Whenever they turn up on our doorstep, either Billy or I go with them. Make sure they're not breaking any laws or endangering the waters. Though, this should be an easy one. A family, which doesn't guarantee anything, but the dad is a professor from the mainland, his kids are in college, the daughter is a marine biology major and the son some kind of computer whiz. They think they can find the wreck of the Isadora."

"That's just legend."

"Who am I to burst their bubble?" Nick shrugged.

Kenny held back a chuckle. "Well, if you need a hand."

Squinting at his old friend for a long minute, Nick nodded. "You never know. I might take you up on that."

Kenny patted him on the shoulder. "At your disposal."

A few more friendly words were exchanged and the co-owner with Billy Everrett of the Big Island Dive shop, keeping his arm around his wife's waist, exited the restaurant.

That was what she wanted some day. A love that would last through the years, all of the ups and downs. Just like Doug and Emily, Nick and Kara, and Billy and Angela. Some days, she thought maybe tomorrow would be her turn. Other days, she thought every good man on the planet was taken. Then there were days like today, when she wondered if her Navy knight in shining armor was going to turn into the proverbial toad. After all, for her, they always did.

CHAPTER TEN

I f Kenny checked his watch one more time, the thing would probably shout back at him to get a grip. He'd checked out of the hotel this morning and taken his gear to Nick's old apartment over the Surf Up Saloon. Nick's previous tenants had moved out a couple of days ago and the cleaning crew had finally come through.

His challenge for the day was it was still only one o'clock in the afternoon and he had nothing to do for two hours until he picked Sara up at the hotel. Having fully unpacked, and not wanting to check out the downtown decorations without Sara, he opted to kill a little time at the dive shop. Pulling into the parking lot, he looked up at the sign and smiled. Giving up the Navy had been a tough decision, but it became easier when he realized that retiring didn't mean he'd have to give up the water.

Pushing the door open, the place was quiet, except for a radio playing a local Hawaiian station. Kenny nodded to Lexi behind the counter.

"Well, look who the cat dragged in!" The dive shop manager set her pen on a pad of paper, and hopping off her seat, hurried up to Kenny for a hug that only an old friend could offer.

"Good to see you too."

Lexi chuckled and stepped back. "Nick mentioned you were in town for a bit. I was starting to wonder if you were going to come say hello or if we were going to have to go looking for you."

"That wouldn't be too hard." Billy came out from the back room. "He's been keeping company with Sara Alani."

Lexi's brows shot up high. "Really?"

Lord. He really did not like lying to his friends, but if this pretense was going to work with the families, it had to be just their little secret. "She's a nice girl."

"No one is going to argue with you over that one!" Billy slapped him on the back. "You joining us for a dive today?"

Kenny shook his head. "Another time. Just popping in to say hello before heading out for some Christmas shopping."

The bell above the door chimed as a family tumbled through the entrance like a small hurricane of enthusiasm. Kenny pegged them as related within seconds—they all shared the same animated gestures and that particular brand of barely contained excitement that suggested they were having the time of their lives.

The patriarch, a man in his late fifties with Einstein hair and cargo shorts, made a beeline for the counter. "Aloha! We're here for the long-term rental gear we reserved. Name's Thorne."

"Nice to meet you, Professor." Lexi stepped away from Kenny and extended her hand to the smiling man.

"This is my wife, Abigail, my son Kurt, and daughter Chloe."

Kenny's gaze swept the group. No doubt the family Nick had mentioned at dinner last night. Two younger versions of the professor—Kurt and Chloe—both in their early twenties who'd inherited his wild hair but thankfully not his fashion sense, were already examining equipment with the focused intensity of people who actually knew what they were looking at. Definitely fit the description of Marine Biology major and computer whiz.

Beside the man, a slender woman with golden shoulder length hair in white slacks and neatly pressed peach button down shirt, noticed Kenny and smiled politely. He had to smother a smile. The man appeared to be the typical absent minded professor but his wife beside him looked like she'd fallen off a magazine cover for what to wear when you're over forty and still look smashing.

"We weren't expecting you until tomorrow morning." Lexi held her smile. "Nick, your captain, is just finishing up some of the list you gave him."

"Wonderful." The older man pulled out some rolled papers from a pouch slung over his shoulder. "I wanted to go over a few last minute things with him. Is he available?"

"Not right now, unfortunately." Lexi glanced at Billy. "Perhaps Billy can help you?"

Not losing any of his enthusiasm, the man unrolled the papers on the counter, but his son was the one to step forward. "We've been doing a little last minute math, and now that we're here, we suspect we might have to shift our coordinates a bit."

The daughter nodded. "My suspicions are that we overestimated some of the silt shift." She pointed to a spot on the map. "Instead of starting tomorrow's dive here." Her finger slid a short distance to the east on the map. "We'd like to start here."

Lexi studied the map with Billy looking over her shoulder.

Nodding his head, Billy took a step back. "If that's what you folks would like, I don't see any problem with it."

"Perfect." The man beamed at them. "Then we'll see you in the morning."

As the family practically bounced out the shop door, Kenny's phone buzzed with a text from Sara.

Getting off early. Can you pick me up in twenty?

Absolutely. Slipping his phone into his pocket, he glanced up at Billy and Lexi. "Have to run. I'll be curious to hear how tomorrow goes."

Billy nodded. "So are we."

Knowing they would be going shopping today, she'd changed out of her uniform and eagerly waited for him by the service entrance. Purse slung over her shoulder, Sara spotted Kenny's rental car pulling into the hotel parking lot and smoothed the front of her capris then tucked a stray strand of hair behind her ear. She was feeling ridiculously like a teenager waiting for a first date, which was absurd since this wasn't a real date. It was a mission. An operation. At least, that's what she kept telling herself.

Hurrying to the curb, she was delighted when Kenny hopped out of the car and circled round to the passenger side.

"You look lovely." Kenny held the car door as she slid into the passenger seat.

"Thank you." She buckled in and suddenly she was looking forward to this afternoon more than she had realized.

"I'll tell you a secret." He clicked his seat belt into place and flashed a dazzling smile at her. "I'm a terrible shopper."

For a moment, she'd held her breath, not sure if she was going to like what he had to say, but she exhaled on a laugh. "I don't know if that's much of a secret."

"You know?" His brows lifted higher than his sunglasses.

She shrugged. "For one thing, you've mentioned it before, but honestly, I've never met a man who liked shopping, never mind was any good at it. It's why women used to get toasters and vacuum cleaners as birthday gifts for decades. Fortunately for you... I love shopping, especially at Christmas."

Kenny pulled onto the main drag and flashed that bright smile at her again. "That's what I was counting on."

Down the road a short way, she raised her hand and pointed. "Turn left at the next light. We're going to hit some of my favorite shops first."

Already, downtown Kona sizzled with a cheerful tangle of festive energy. The air smelled of salt, plumeria, and the sweet scent of roasting nuts from street vendors' carts. Lights twinkled from palm trees, streetlights, and storefront windows, transforming the small town into a tropical Christmas wonderland.

Easing into a row of angled parking spots along the main street, Kenny looked at the first window and whistled. "Okay,"

"Have you never been here at Christmas before?"

He shook his head.

"Well then, you're in for a treat. Everyone should experience Kona Christmas Kitsch."

"Say again?"

She hopped out of the car. "Kitsch. Colorful and whimsical decorations and gifts that reflect tropical and Hawaiian themes."

"O-kay." Head tipped to one side, Kenny eyed the first window.

"And that is Kitsch." A Santa Claus, complete with beard and red coat, balanced on a neon green surfboard while a mechanical wave looped behind him.

"I've seen a lot of things in my life," smiling, he shook his head, "but that may top the list."

"You mean you've never seen Surfing Santa before?" She couldn't contain her amusement.

"I've seen Santas. I've seen surfers." He continued to turn his head from side to side. "But never, in all my visits to the islands have I ever seen them together. At least not sober."

"So you've seen surfing Santas after a few drinks?"

"No. Maybe a pink elephant or two," he joked.

"We might find a pink turtle or two, but I doubt we'll find any elephants." She slipped her hand into the crook of his arm and urged him forward. "Let's go inside and see what we can find. If we can't find anything for Maile here, there are a slew of other shops we can check out."

Inside, Kenny found an ornament similar to the large surfing Santa in the window complete with a lei around his neck and sunglasses. He held it up as if he were examining a diamond in the light.

"Like it?"

"It's different. Definitely screams Christmas in Hawaii."

"That it does," she agreed. "Thinking of it for yourself or someone on your list?"

"Actually," he set it back on the rack, "I was wondering why would anyone want to straddle a sliver of wood on the ocean when with a pair of goggles they could be in the *water*."

"Sliver of wood? You mean the surfboards?"

He nodded.

"Do you mean to tell me that you've never been surfing?"

"Nope."

"That's like… like visiting Italy and never eating pasta. Or going to France and avoiding wine." Sara shook her head in amazement.

"I thought SEALs could do anything in the water, on the water, by the water, maybe even walk on water."

One brow cocked high and he pinned her with those beautiful baby blues. "Anything, huh?"

Suddenly heat filled her cheeks as she realized that maybe she could have phrased that a little better.

"Sorry," he took a step back, "I'm sure there are plenty of SEALs who have surfed, I'm just not one of them."

She reached for the ornament he'd put back in place and held it up in front of him. "We have to fix this."

"We do?"

"Absolutely. It's un-Hawaiian not to surf. I think, sailor, it's way past time someone got you on a surf board."

"Someone?"

"Well, as fate would have it, pretty much anyone born and raised on these islands knows how to ride a surfboard and I am willing to stake a year's income that teaching you how is going to be way more fun than shopping."

CHAPTER ELEVEN

The idea of standing on a surfboard and riding a wave to the beach had never appealed to Kenny. Not till now. It had been a few days since he and Sara had gone shopping. Who knew picking out ornaments for all his friends could be so much fun. Then again, he knew the gifts had little to do with the fun day. No, his good mood had everything to do with the company.

Since their little shopping escapade, Sara had worked not only the day shift, but picked up a couple of extra evening shifts working the restrooms. Waiting for her to finally have time off so they could go back to their fake dates had been more challenging for him than he'd expected. One thing that every Navy SEAL learned early on in their career was the benefits of patience. It was right up there with observing every detail, retaining the data, and using it to stay alive. Except in this case, patience was in short supply. It surprised him just how much he was looking forward to her day off and their little surfing lesson.

Pulling up to her house, he barely had the car in park before Sara came jogging out the front door, a wide, sun-drenched smile on her face. She was already dressed for the part in board shorts and a long-sleeved rash guard, her red hair pulled back in a practical ponytail.

Driving away from the curb, Kenny caught a glimpse of the familiar twitch of curtains in the front window. "Our audience is still watching."

"Always. Mom probably has the binoculars out by now." Sara directed him toward a beach north of town. "We're going to Kahalu'u. It's perfect for learning—sandy bottom, gentle waves, and not too crowded this time of day."

The drive took about fifteen minutes. Along the way, Kenny found himself studying the water. From his military training, he automatically assessed conditions—wind direction, wave height, current patterns. The waves looked manageable, maybe three feet at most, rolling in with steady rhythm.

"I've arranged to borrow a couple of boards from my cousin Kai. Park next to his truck." Sara pointed at a simple white van with a man he presumed to be her cousin standing beside it, his hair and skin bronzed from years in the sun, his gaze on their car as they drove up. Two long, thick surfboards leaned against the van's side. They looked less like the sleek "slivers of wood" he'd imagined and more like buoyant, foam-covered rescue craft.

They unloaded the boards—longer and wider than Kenny had expected—and Sara led him to a shaded spot under a palm tree. The beach was relatively quiet, with only a few other surfers in the water and some families scattered along the sand.

"Meet your new best friend," Sara patted one of the boards. It was at least nine feet long. "This is a foamie. It's stable, forgiving, and won't knock your teeth out when it hits you in the head."

"Reassuring," Kenny noted dryly.

"See those waves? They're breaking perfectly. Not too fast, not too slow."

"Fast and slow. Got it." Not that he had any clue what would be too fast or too slow...for water. "Do the sharks know this too?"

Her eyes narrowed making her whole face crinkle in confusion. She looked absolutely adorable, and then it hit her he was teasing. Sort of. Rolling her eyes and shaking her head, she pointed at the sand. "This is your classroom. Rule one: respect the ocean. Rule two: it's going to win, so learn how to fall. First lesson," Sara laid one board flat on the sand, "we're going to practice on land before we get wet. Lie down on the board like you're paddling."

Kenny felt slightly ridiculous lying on a surfboard in the sand, but he followed Sara's instructions. He felt her hands on his ribs and hips, adjusting his position, and nearly bit his tongue trying to ignore the gentle touch against his skin.

"You need to find the sweet spot. Too far back and the nose pops up, you stall. Too far forward and you nosedive. You'll feel it when you're in the water.

"Hands flat, about where your chest is. When you feel the wave catch you, you're going to push up and swing your feet under you in one motion." Sara demonstrated the movement in slow motion. "It's called a pop-up. Try it."

Kenny pushed himself up and attempted to bring his feet forward. He managed to get upright, though his stance was awkward.

"Not bad for a first try. But you're thinking too much. It needs to be one fluid movement." Sara demonstrated again. "Military training probably helps with the upper body strength, but surfing is about flow, not force."

They practiced the pop-up several more times until Kenny could execute it smoothly. Then Sara showed him proper stance—feet perpendicular to the board, knees bent, arms out for balance.

"Remember, the board goes where you look. Look toward shore, not down at the water." Sara picked up her board. "Ready to get wet?"

The water was warm, warmer than Kenny had expected. They waded out to waist-deep water, boards in tow. Sara positioned him carefully. And again, he did his best to ignore the feel of her hands on his skin.

She held his board steady as a small wave rolled under them. "Feel that?"

Swallowing hard, he nodded. What more could he do?

"That's what you're looking for. When you feel the wave lift the back of your board, start paddling hard. I'll give you a push to help you catch it."

He stretched out on the board, chest pressed to fiberglass, arms cutting the water. The smell of salt, the push and pull of the swell—it felt different from swimming, different from diving. Exposed. Upright. Like surrendering control instead of commanding it. Not since his first days of SEAL training had he been so awkward and off-balance and most of that had little to do with the water.

"Here it comes!" Sara's voice cut sharp and bright. "Three…two…one—up!"

The wave approached, lifting the tail of his board. He started paddling as Sara had instructed, feeling her hands on the back of the board giving him a push. Suddenly the wave caught him and he was gliding forward, the board carrying him toward shore.

"Pop up!" she shouted from behind him.

Kenny moved. Palms planted, chest lifting, feet sliding under. The board wobbled but held as the wave shoved him forward. Spray stung his face. For three glorious seconds, he stood riding the water like he'd been born to it—until the nose dipped, momentum surged, and he toppled headfirst into the surf.

Salt water filled his mouth. He surfaced sputtering, slicking his hair back from his eyes.

Sara's laugh rang out, clear as a bell. "Not bad for a first try!"

He pushed the board back toward her, grinning despite himself. "Again."

Because now that he'd had a taste of it—three seconds of impossible flight—he wanted more.

For the next hour, Kenny threw himself into learning with the same intensity he'd brought to every other challenge in his life. He caught wave after wave, each ride lasting a little longer than the one before. Sara stayed beside him, offering encouragement and adjustments, her enthusiasm infectious.

By the time they finally took a break, Kenny had managed several rides all the way to shore. He was exhausted, exhilarated, and covered in sand, but he couldn't remember the last time he'd had this much fun learning something completely new. Or maybe it wasn't something new at all, but something new with Sara.

Digging her toes into the warm sand, Sara laughed out loud for the umpteenth time today. This time not just at Kenny's awkward wipeout but at the way he came up, hair slicked back and grinning like a little boy experiencing his first Christmas morning.

Sara felt something flutter in her chest that had nothing to do with the ocean breeze. This was supposed to be part of their fake relationship, another performance for anyone who might see them together. But there was nothing fake about the way her pulse quickened when Kenny smiled at her like that.

When she'd adjusted his stance earlier, her hands had rested against the hard planes of muscle along his ribs, his hip. Just a touch, nothing more, but she'd felt the strength beneath his skin, steady and unyielding. The memory still tingled in her palms, the brief, practical contact had thrown her off balance more than any wave. Over the years she'd corrected plenty of new surfers, but none of them had made her heart trip over itself. And what the heck was she supposed to do with that? Kenny would only be here for a short while. The man was supposed to be nothing more than a pretend boyfriend to keep her mother happy and give her a relaxed, peaceful holiday season. And yet—standing there, surfboard planted in the sand beside him, looking at her with a boyish mix of triumph and mischief—she couldn't deny it had been a long time since she'd had this much fun or felt such a strong connection. If she wasn't more careful, falling off a surfboard would be the least of her problems. She needed to put some space between them, get back on the solid ground of their arrangement before she did something stupid, like stand toe to toe and kiss that impish grin off his face. Taking a step back, she brushed sand from hands as if that were all that was needed to brush away the attraction churning inside her. "We should probably rinse off and get these boards back to Kai."

"Yes, ma'am." Kenny nodded, grabbing one of the

towels she'd brought. "I need to swing by the dive shop anyway. Have to check in with Nick about tagging along with some new clients of his."

They loaded the boards back onto her cousin's van, shouting their thanks to Kai, who gave them a lazy wave from where he stood with his own board at his side. The public rinse-off station was a simple outdoor shower head. As they took turns washing the salt and sand from their skin and hair, Sara tried very hard not to notice the way the water sluiced over Kenny's broad shoulders and down his back. This charade was definitely getting more complicated than she'd expected.

Walking back to his car, toweling their hair dry, she searched for something safe to talk about. "For a guy who's never surfed, you're not half bad."

"All credit goes to the teacher." He opened the passenger door for her. The gentlemanly gesture felt so ingrained in him, so automatic, it made her appreciate him all the more.

The drive to the dive shop was quiet and comfortable. She found herself replaying his wipeouts in her head, not with smug satisfaction, but with a growing respect for his persistence. He hadn't gotten frustrated or embarrassed. He'd simply assessed the failure, corrected, and tried again. A SEAL through and through.

Kenny pulled into the parking lot of the Big Island Dive Shop, the familiar sign a welcome sight. Inside, the faint hum of the air conditioners welcomed them.

"Look what the tide brought in," Billy called out from behind the counter, a knowing grin spreading across his face. His gaze flicked from a sandy, salt-streaked Kenny to her. "Having fun on your day off?"

The question was innocent enough, but the look in his eyes made Sara feel a flush of heat creep up her neck. For the first time, she felt a pang of guilt over their deception. Billy was her friend, and here she was, playing a part. But then Kenny's hand was on the small of her back, a light, casual touch that was both for show and, she suspected, for support, and a tiny part deep down hoped maybe even for real—and wasn't that dangerous territory to be wandering in. "We had a great time." She hoped her voice sounded more casual than she felt. "Kenny's a fast learner."

Billy's grin widened. "I'll bet he is."

Just then, Lexi walked into the shop from the back office. "Just got off the phone with Steve at the marina. You'll never guess whose boat pulled into a rented slip in the middle of the night."

Wiping grease off his hands on a towel, brows buckled, Nick came through the doors from the warehouse.

Lexi didn't wait for guesses. "Julian Vance."

Stopping in his tracks, Nick's frown deepened. "What is that snake doing here?"

Sara had no idea who this person was or why they called him a snake, but from the way the staff at the shop all glanced each other, they certainly knew.

"The Thornes?" Billy asked even though she suspected it was more of an answer than a question.

On a sigh, Nick tossed the dirty rag onto the counter. "Is the pope Catholic?"

"Is this Vance character going to be a problem?" Every muscle in Kenny's body seemed to tighten as if he were a hound dog on a mission.

Nick shook his head. "If we're all lucky, that modern day pirate is just passing through on his way to being someone else's headache."

None of that sounded good to Sara. She could see the way the men looked at each other and could almost see the silent conversation. If she were a betting woman, she'd wager this is how they communicated when they were all active duty together.

Just then, her cell buzzed and she glanced down at the phone. Quickly reading the text, her gaze shifted to meet Kenny's. "That's Maria, her son is running a fever. She wants to know if I can take her shift tonight. Is it okay if we do a rain check on dinner?"

"Of course. Tomorrow we can play in my world."

"Your world?" She hadn't meant for her voice to crack.

His grin widened. "Today we played on your water.

Tomorrow, we play under mine."

A happy smile replaced the moment of panic that had tickled her spine. "I can do that." And she could. Anyone who had grown up with these water rats could handle her own over or under the water. "Works for me."

"I'd better get you home so you can change for work." Kenny waved at his buddies, not saying another word about the late night visitor, and gently placing his hand once again at the small of her back, ushered her out the door.

The simple touch, along with all the playful teasing made her stomach twist and flip. The line between their fake relationship and whatever reality they were sharing had never felt more blurred.

CHAPTER TWELVE

"So, what do you think?"

Holding the cell phone to her ear with one hand and the kitchen curtains slightly askew with the other, Missy sighed. "I honestly don't know. What has it been, a week?"

"Is that all?" Maile Everrett huffed over the phone. "Feels longer to me. Maybe I should hang some extra mistletoe around."

"Won't work. I've got some hanging from every chandelier and every doorway but they never come in to have a reason to stand under it."

"So now what?"

Missy shook her head even though her best friend couldn't see. "Ooh, here he is."

"And?"

"Well, hang on."

"I'm leaving, Mom." Sara called from the hall. "We'll be with Nick and the gang. If you need me, call the dive shop."

Her hand over the cell phone, she called back to her daughter. "Have fun sweetie."

"Well?" Maile asked.

"Hang on. She's only halfway down the walkway."

"What's he doing?"

"Holding the door open for her."

"Oh. That's my Kenny. All my son's friends are such nice boys."

"Boys?" Missy momentarily tore her gaze away from the curb and glanced at the phone, before returning to her viewing stance. "Oh, he's kissing her."

"Kissing how?"

"What do you mean how?" Again she glanced down at her phone.

"On the cheek? The mouth? Holding her or not? Politely or should we call get a room?"

"Maile!"

"You know what I mean."

"Okay. Oh." She couldn't help smiling. "One arm around her waist. Leaning in. Brief kiss on the lips."

"Then why are you sighing?"

"Maile, you should see how he's looking at her."

"Take a picture."

"Too late. They're getting into the car. His eyes lasered in on hers, the corners of his mouth curled in a sweet smile, and it took him a minute to let go. Oh, Maile. I think we finally got this one right!"

It had taken every inch of self control Kenny had to pull away from Sara. The moment he'd hopped out of the car, he'd spotted that wavering curtain, this time in what he knew to be the kitchen window. By the time Sara reached him, she'd confirmed his suspicions that mama Alani was doing some pretty sloppy recon. With silent agreement, he'd pulled her in for a delicate and friendly kiss.

The moment his fingers curled around her waist, he'd known something had shifted in him. When his lips touched hers, the desire to pull her even closer and not let go was possibly the most frightening sensation he'd ever encountered. Only years of SEAL training allowed him to follow through on his mission without totally mucking up their deal.

"You all right?" Sara's voice sounded small, worried.

"Sorry. Just thinking."

"About?" Her fingers twisted together in her lap. "I mean, if this whole arrangement is taking up too much of your time, we don't have to—"

"No." He had to work hard to keep that single syllable from coming out loud and desperate. "No. My mind was just wandering. It started with your mother at the curtains, then it jumped to I haven't seen much of your dad, then it stuttered to a halt when you showed up at the door."

Her cheeks tinted rose and her lashes lowered a moment. "Thank you."

Instantly, his mind drifted to the few times she'd mentioned her dating history. It struck him like a snowball in the face on an icy day that not many men had told her how beautiful she was unless they wanted something from her. Anger simmered under the surface and he found himself wanting very badly to make her happy. "Did I tell you that once, just before BUDs, I actually considered proposing?"

Bashful blue eyes widened in surprise before she silently shook her head.

He turned the corner and decided if there was a sliver of a chance that his attraction was more than hormonal, honesty would be the best policy. "Kathy Delaney. Tall, blonde, with legs that went on forever."

"Ah, so you're a leg man."

"Sometimes." He smiled. "She was sweet and brassy all at the same time. We had a lot of…fun together."

The way her one brow lifted, he suspected she understood what he meant.

"We'd talked about future plans like most people. A house, kids, a dog, maybe a cat. Would that house be by the water or the mountains. Big or small. In theory, we'd agreed on a nice family home."

"I sense a but coming."

"Yeah." He sighed. "The reality was that my first wife was the Navy. My missions were long, and often secretive, and staying behind waiting for me to return to go on a movie date wasn't as romantic as she'd thought it would be."

"I'm sorry."

He shook his head. "Don't be. She married an insurance salesman and I realized that I had no business asking any woman to wait for me to come home, praying it wasn't in a coffin." He held up his hand. "And before you say I'm sorry again, the most unexpected thing was not being upset when she broke it off. I mean, my pride took a hit, but not my heart."

Sara shifted in her seat, her smile almost self deprecating. "I actually know what you mean. I gave and gave and gave because I thought my relationship with Vinny mattered, and then I realized one day, that the only thing that would be hurt if we broke up was my pride."

Unable to resist, he reached across the console, took hold of her hand, and squeezed. He didn't say anything, neither did she. How many people had he known in his life, where so much could be said with so few words?

When they pulled into the dive shop parking lot, Kenny was still holding her hand. The silent connection gave her a sense of comfort and strength. How she wished things could be different, real. As usual, Kenny opened the door for her. Both the car and the dive shop. She was getting used to this old fashioned chivalry. Rejoining the dating world after this Christmas was not going to be easy.

"Oh, good." Lexi looked up from her regular perch behind the main counter. "Billy's been waiting for you. There's been a bit of a glitch in today's plans."

"Did Emily not bring her gear?" Since Sara and Emily were the same size, and even though she'd grown up diving with the Everretts, Sara had never found the spare money to invest in her own gear.

"Oh, she did." Lexi waved her thumb over her shoulder toward the warehouse behind them at the same moment Billy came out.

"Oh good." Billy grinned up at them.

"I'm starting to wonder." Kenny drilled him with a serious stare.

Billy shook his head. "We had a boat limp back to the

docks this morning. Doug is working on finding the problem, but that means we don't have a spare boat for diving today."

"Oh." Sara didn't realize until now how much she'd been looking forward to sharing this part of Kenny's world with him.

Hands in front of him, Billy smiled at Sara. "We've got a fix. Nick asked the Thornes if they'd mind having a Navy SEAL share the boat with them."

"And?" Kenny was still staring oddly at Billy.

"They love the idea of having a big bad SEAL on their boat. If you can't trust Uncle Sam's elite, who can you trust?"

"Mm," was all Kenny said.

"They're at the docks waiting for you." Either Billy hadn't noticed the steady glare Kenny threw his way, or he didn't care. Sara, on the other hand, was curious to know what was going on. "Let's get all the gear in the back of the car and you two can be on your merry way."

"Merry," Kenny muttered.

Two seconds later, as the guys were hefting the bags of diving gear over their shoulders, Sara saw their heads locked together, their voices low and inaudible from this distance. Then Kenny nodded. Something was most definitely up.

All the gear loaded in the car, and the two of them buckled in, Sara waited for Kenny to pull out of the parking lot before facing him. "Care to tell me what that little tete a tete was all about?"

"You noticed." His stern expression gave way to a slight smile.

She bobbed her head.

"That Julian Vance character's boat hasn't moved on. They're hovering around Kona."

"And that's a problem?"

He shrugged. "Maybe, maybe not."

"Why maybe? I gather they're treasure hunters, like the Thornes."

"Not just hunters. Poachers."

"Poachers? As in illegally killing animals kind of poachers."

"Illegally pilfering sunken treasure. They sneak in and scoop up what they can when no one is looking. They come in droves once a serious treasure hunter stakes a claim, but these guys have a reputation for trouble, and Nick doesn't like that they're hovering so close. He wants extra eyes."

She bobbed her head and twisted forward in her seat. "Then he has two extra sets."

That sweet smile widened and if she knew him better, she'd swear she saw a hint of pride in his eyes.

It didn't take long to reach the marina where the dive shop kept their boats. As soon as she stepped out of the car, her gaze landed on two women giggling across the way. "Oh, hell."

"What?" Kenny's head snapped up, his eyes already scanning their surroundings.

"Mary Louise Fletcher. One of the mean girls in high school and she's not improved much with age."

"I see." His gaze remained fixed on the two young women, swinging strappy sandals from their fingers, strutting in bikinis that barely covered what God gave them, and giggling like a couple of drunken school girls at their first frat party.

"Sara!" Mary Louise strutted up to her, taking her time to look Kenny over from head to toe and back. "This can't be the new man in your life your mother has been telling the whole island about?"

And here it went.

Before Sara could open her mouth, Kenny came around beside her and looped his arm around her waist, tugging her in closer. Glancing down, he leveled his gaze with hers, drank her in with his eyes as if she were a well of fresh water in a barren desert, then turned to face the two women staring at them with their jaws hanging open. "So nice to meet some of Sara's friends."

It took everything in her not to choke at that. Hiding her amusement with her hand, she cleared her throat and introduced everyone.

Easing away from her side, Kenny leaned over, kissed her soundly on the lips, and then, once again, locked gazes with hers. "I'll get our gear, take it down to the boat."

All Sara could do was nod. That kiss had left her lips seared as if she'd been branded with a hot iron.

The three of them watched the man stroll across the lot and down the ramp. Sara almost sighed.

"Wow." Peggy Martin actually fanned herself. "Your mother did not exaggerate."

"I'd say she under delivered." Mary Louise was still staring at Kenny as he loaded the gear onto the boat.

"Well, ladies," Sara had somehow managed to pull herself together, "I don't want to keep Kenny waiting. Have a nice day." Swinging her purse over her shoulder, she waved at the two women still standing in the middle of the lot and doing her best effort at sashaying, made her way to Kenny's side, eased up on her tiptoes, and gently kissed him on the lips. Then she softly whispered, "Thank you."

Dropping the bag he held in one hand, he circled his arms around her, lowered his lips to hers, and huskily responded, "any time," seconds before touching her lips with his and making her toes curl. If Mary Louise and Peggy were still watching, Kenny had just given them one hell of a performance.

CHAPTER THIRTEEN

That kiss at the marina should have been for show. A calculated move to silence the high school mean girls and solidify the cover story for his friends. But as Kenny stood on the deck of the Thornes' chartered boat, the memory of her lips on his was a distraction he hadn't planned for. He'd told himself it was just part of the mission, but the Senior Chief in him knew a compromised objective when he saw one. And right now, his objectivity where Sara Alani was concerned was completely shot.

He forced his attention outward, his gaze sweeping the horizon in a practiced, automatic scan. Professor Thorne was excitedly explaining his search grid theory to Sara, who listened with a genuine interest that seemed to put the whole family at ease. The Thorne kids were double-checking their dive computers with a quiet competence Kenny could respect. They were professionals.

Off to one side of the table he spotted Mrs. Thorne, over a drop cloth, chipping away at a pile of conglomerate rock, no doubt hopeful to find a treasure imbedded in the sediment formations. Beside her there were a few loose old iron nails and something that looked like it might have been a copper button. The more interesting item, a single odd shaped coin, silver, and from his inexperienced eye, very damn old.

"I saw that yesterday." Chloe beamed up at him. "I spotted the darkened sand, started fanning the way Dad taught me as a kid. As soon as I picked it up, I knew it was the real thing. First time we've actually found something that shows we're on the right track. I just know the San Isidro is down here. Close."

"Now, Chloe," her dad patted her shoulder, "the date is very promising, but—"

"I know," Chloe sighed.

"Ooh. Is that what I think it is?" In her formfitting wetsuit already, Sara stood beside him. "So you found what you're looking for?"

"Maybe. According to the manifests and other documents Dad and Kurt have tracked down, the San Isidro should be carrying a motherload of treasure. Not just a few coins."

Now Kurt appeared beside them. "We figure yesterday's treasures were a bounce site."

"What's a bounce site?" Sara asked.

"Just like it sounds. Probably where a ship bounced, hit, while tossed about by the sea. The actual wreck is most likely somewhere else... not far. If my calculations are right, the wreck should be in this new area." The kid raised his gaze to the horizon and Kenny followed looking in the same direction.

Then he saw it. A ship a few miles off their port side. Far enough to not be an issue. Close enough to monitor what the Thornes were doing. And if Nick and Billy were correct, that boat belonged to Julian Vance. They weren't even trying to be subtle. It was a lazy, arrogant shadow, and every instinct in Kenny's body went on high alert.

Leaning beside him, Sara followed his gaze, her easy smile faltering slightly. "That's them?"

He nodded. "Looks like it."

Her eyes met his, and in them he saw not fear or concern, but a flicker of shared purpose. She gave a small, sharp nod, and in that silent exchange, she wasn't just his fake date anymore. She was his partner on this dive.

The plan was simple: the Thornes would search their designated grid near the reef drop-off, and he and Sara would dive the area, take in the scenery, and keep an eye open, just in case.

As he geared up, the familiar clicks of buckles and the hiss of regulators grounded him. This was his world. Sara checked her divers watch, her wrist compass, and the gauges on her tanks before strapping her diver's knife onto her calf. Had any woman ever looked so beautiful? He hefted her tanks, helped her secure them, then gave a thumbs-up, and she returned it, her eyes bright with anticipation above her regulator. With a nod, she executed a smooth back roll from the rail and headed down.

For Kenny, dropping beneath the surface was like entering another dimension. The noisy world of wind and engines vanished, replaced by a profound, muffled silence broken only by the rhythmic sound of his own breathing. Sunlight pierced the turquoise water in shifting, golden shafts, illuminating a world of impossible beauty. Schools of sun-yellow tangs streamed past them like liquid confetti. A majestic green sea turtle drifted by with ancient indifference. Below them, a sprawling tapestry of coral in a hundred shapes and colors teemed with life.

He kept Sara in his peripheral vision at all times. She moved through the water with the effortless grace of someone who'd been born to it, her red hair a vibrant flag in the electric blue. He swam slightly above and behind her, a position that gave him a clear view of her and their surroundings. It was a habit born from years of watching his teammates' backs, but with Sara, it felt different. It felt personal.

She caught his eye and pointed, her gloved finger indicating a grumpy-looking puffer fish trying to hide under a ledge. When it puffed up indignantly, she brought her hands to her mask in a gesture of mock surprise, bubbles escaping her regulator in a short burst that looked suspiciously like a laugh. He couldn't help but smile. Here, in the silent beauty of his world, her playful spirit was just as captivating. This was what it felt like, he realized. Their two worlds, his and hers, melding perfectly—too bad it was time to ascend. He gestured with his thumb to the surface, and with a nod, the two slowly made their way toward the light. If he had his druthers, this day would never end.

Breaking the surface felt like leaving a cathedral. Sara pulled her regulator from her mouth and treaded water beside Kenny, both of them blinking in the sudden brightness of the afternoon sun.

"That was incredible," her voice carried across the calm water to where the Thornes waited on their boat.

One by one, they climbed the boat's ladder, the sudden weight of their tanks a grounding reality. On deck, Sara and Kenny shed their tanks and BCDs, the familiar routine of post-dive gear management giving Sara time to process what she'd just experienced. Diving with Kenny had felt different from any dive she'd done before. The way he'd positioned himself slightly above and behind her, always keeping her in sight, had made her feel protected without being crowded. Professional, but personal.

Mrs. Thorne appeared with a plate of fresh pineapple and mango slices, along with bottles of water. "Fuel up." She flashed a warm smile. "The kids are dying to show you what they brought up."

"Anything interesting down there?" the professor asked, his eyes twinkling like a kid on Christmas morning.

"Just a very grumpy puffer fish and the most beautiful coral I've ever seen," Sara laughed, pulling off her fins and shaking the water from her ears.

"Wait until you see what we found this morning," Chloe called out, her excitement bubbling over.

The professor followed his daughter to the table covered with a towel. Gently lifting the towel, a display of artifacts greeted them.

Sara's breath caught as she took in the collection— pieces of broken pottery, tarnished pewter utensils, and what looked like the remains of a ceramic plate with part of a ship's crest still visible, but even Sara knew not enough of the crest to confirm what ship they'd found.

"This is from the galley." Kurt's voice was tight with excitement.

"The San Isidro," Chloe added, carefully picking up a fragment of pottery. "We're actually looking at pieces from a 300-year-old shipwreck."

"We're not sure of that yet," their father tempered. "It could be any number of ships that sank in this area." The man's stern expression softened. "But if it is, we're going to find the proof."

All heads bobbed and Sara had no doubt this family was going to indeed find what they'd been dreaming of for so long.

Kenny leaned in, studying the artifacts with the same focused attention he brought to everything. "What's the plan now?"

"That's the question." Professor Thorne hovered over his charts. "Time, currents, and storms spread things out, but the main treasure hold should be within a reasonable radius. Tomorrow we're planning to expand our search grid here." With quiet confidence, the man tapped a spot on the chart.

"Looks like our company is getting bored." Abigail Thorne pointed to the departing boat in the distance.

Kenny glanced around, strolled casually to where Nick would have been had he been captaining the boat and returned with a pair of binoculars. Standing in the shade, almost hidden from view, he stared into the distance at the retreating boat.

Not till his let the binoculars fall to his chest did Sara dare approach him. Before she could say a word, his fingers raised to his lip and he reached for a nearby pad of paper and pen. As he leaned against the table, writing, everyone gathered around him. Two words: *Surveillance equipment.*

Once the ship was completely out of sight, Kenny turned to face the family. "I have no idea how Vance knew you were on to the San Isidro site, but that boat has some serious surveillance equipment. The parabolic microphone looks big enough to pick up a pin drop from 300 yards."

"Which is about how far out they were." Professor Thorne looked out toward the poacher's wake.

"I think it's safe to assume they're just waiting to see if you find the motherload." Kenny set the binoculars back where they came from. "But I think we need to have a chat with Billy and Nick. For now, until you find what you're looking for, no verbal commentaries. No mention of nails, or buttons, or dishes. If anything, sound dreary and disappointed. Once you stake your claim, keeping every diver and poacher out for whatever they can steal will be hard enough; keeping this character with his deep pockets and high tech equipment away is a priority."

Everyone nodded. The kids looked at each other before going back to the map they'd been studying.

"Well." Abigail brushed her hands together and lifting her chin, smiled. "I, for one, say let's give that man the performance of a lifetime."

Her husband nodded and both kids looked up from the maps, all three voices echoing, "Agreed."

Sara had to smile at the resilience of this family after the disappointing discovery. Then again, no one chased a treasure for almost a decade if they weren't at least resilient, at best optimists. Kenny came at her side and reached for her hand. She liked that. A lot. Though she had no idea if it was for comfort or for show, for now she was going to enjoy it for as long as she could.

"Can you get tomorrow off?" Kenny spoke so no one else would hear.

She nodded. "Wouldn't miss the show for anything."

A broad smile took over his face. "I figure the more of us on board just having fun, the less serious this could get."

"Do you think?"

His eyes dimmed for a moment. "I hope."

CHAPTER FOURTEEN

Decades of rising before the sun made arriving at the marina at the crack of dawn easy for Kenny. Sara, not so much. When he'd picked her up at the house before the sun had even blinked on the horizon, she'd struggled to keep her eyes open and herself from yawning. Thankfully, he'd thought to stop and pick up a double size of her favorite mocha macchiato with an extra dose of espresso.

Her first sip and she sighed heavily, dipping her head back against the headrest. "Heaven. A gift from the Gods."

Blowing on his fingertips, he brushed them against his shoulder and grinned cheekily at her. "Thank you."

Almost choking on her next sip, she jerked forward, wiped her mouth and turned in his direction. "I meant the coffee."

He chuckled loudly. "I know. You're just so teasible when you're half asleep. Don't you usually get up early to work at the hotel?"

"Not before the sun. Check out is at 11am and most people drag their feet to leave their rooms. Some folks have early flights, but not enough to warrant the entire housekeeping staff report to work at the crack of dawn."

To his surprise, the Thornes were not only at the marina waiting for them, they were all bright eyed and bushytailed, buzzing about like bees in a nest. "Everyone all set?"

Professor and Mrs. Thorne waved from the captain's perch. Unlike the previous days when one of Nick's team had been driving the boat, today Billy himself was manning the boat. Apparently, he wasn't the only one worried about Vance and his intentions.

Standing on deck, with the rising sun winking over the

horizon, and the sea a placid, shimmering blue, it was easy to forget there were bad guys in this world. His gaze fixed on the empty horizon, Vance's boat was nowhere to be seen. After their blatant surveillance yesterday, the sudden absence felt less like a retreat and more like an alarm. Then again, maybe Vance wasn't fond of the crack of dawn either.

"What's the plan?" Sara sidled up beside him. "There's no boat."

He bobbed his head. "Business as usual. If we're lucky, they found another dangling carrot to chase and the Thornes can continue and we can enjoy the day."

"That would be nice."

"I have to take some photographs, mark the area, document the finds and locations." Chloe was already suited up and ready for her morning dive. "Kurt and I are going to head down. Dad will spot. We'll see you later."

Again, he glanced at the horizon, with no sign of Vance's boat, he nodded and his hand at Sara's back, nudged her toward their equipment. The sooner he got down there to keep an eye on the young Thornes, the better he'd feel. An enemy you can see is a problem; an enemy you can't is a threat.

"Do you think they got bored and went home?" Mrs. Thorne asked from the railing by the dive platform where her children had just rolled into the water.

"Maybe." He smiled at the woman.

When she walked away to join her husband, Sara leaned closer. "Do you really think so?"

"Not a chance," Kenny turned to help her with her tanks. "Men like Vance don't get bored. They get patient."

The simple act of securing her gear, the familiar clicks of the buckles and the weight of the tank settling on her back, felt routine. But the brief moment his hands brushed her shoulders was anything but. He pulled his gloves on with a sharp snap, forcing his mind back to the mission. The Thornes were already in the water, their excitement a tangible energy in the air.

"Ready?" he asked, his voice all business.

Sara met his gaze over her regulator, her eyes bright and clear. She gave a sharp nod. Together, they executed a back roll off the side, the cool embrace of the ocean a welcome shock that instantly cleared his head.

The world below was a comforting blanket of light and color. Golden shafts of sun pierced the surface, illuminating schools of parrotfish that flashed like jewels against the sprawling, intricate architecture of the reef. Sea fans waved gracefully in the current. Fish startled by the intrusion darted away. He watched Sara move through the water, her movements fluid and confident. Her pleasure in the life around her a joy to watch. He fell into his familiar position—slightly above and behind her, a silent, watchful guardian. It was a role he'd played a thousand times, but with her, the stakes felt infinitely higher.

They swam toward the galley site, the energy of the reef life giving way to a more somber, quiet landscape. A short distance away, Kurt and Chloe were already working, their movements slow and methodical. Then, Kenny saw Chloe stop. She hung suspended in the water for a moment, waving Kurt to her side. The two focused on something nearby. Kurt shook his head and then turned, signaling for Kenny to join them as Chloe held the camera, clicking away.

When they reached the kids, the peaceful beauty of the dive shattered. The delicate, sandy bottom resembled the remnants of a kid's sand castle washed away by the tide. Lumps where there shouldn't be, holes where there shouldn't be, fragile, ancient coral heads were shattered, their white skeletons a stark violation against the blue. This had all the earmarks of a smash-and-grab.

He caught Sara's eye; her own were wide with anger. Without another signal needed, he jerked his thumb toward the surface. The dive was over.

Back on the boat, the silence was heavy, broken only by the clank of gear being set on the deck. Staring at the images on her daughter's camera, Abigail shook her head. "Why?"

Kenny stripped off his BCD and walked to the bow,

needing a moment of separation before he made the call. Billy at his side, he punched in Nick's number.

"They were here. And they weren't gentle. Who knows what they found—or if they'll be back."

Nick swore, a low, sharp sound. "That explains the call I just got. A buddy down at the marina says Vance hired a couple of local divers this morning. Let's just say, these guys aren't known for their ethics. The kind of guys brought in when there's no concern over collateral damage."

The pieces clicked into place with sickening clarity. Vance wasn't going to be patient and he didn't care who or what got in his way. "We need to start talking about 24/7 site security, and we need it yesterday."

A few more words and Nick promised to get on the extra help ASAP.

The professor stood by his wife, watching the horizon through binoculars. Before Kenny could explain the new development, the professor slowly lowered the binoculars. "Well," his voice quiet and dangerously calm, "it looks like this morning was a bust."

Before anyone could say a word, the man had his fingers to his lips and was scribbling on a piece of paper. "They're back. And they're closing in."

None of this morning had gone the way they'd expected. Until now. Sara kept a casual eye on the boat cutting slowly across the water, its approach both arrogant and predatory. Unlike the previous days when the boat had stopped too far to see, this time the poachers stopped closer than before, but far enough away to maintain a sliver of plausible deniability. The game had begun.

"Well." Hands on her hips, Abigail Thorne projected her voice loud enough to ensure she was heard, but not so loud to be out of place. The lady probably would have done a great job on stage. "That makes two morning dives and nothing to show for it except some worthless pottery chips.

Could we have made a mistake?"

"Mistake? I've spent years following the tides, the storms, calculating." Though the professor's words were harsh, his expression was calm. The man played along beautifully. Running his hand through his hair he stood over the charts. "Maybe I was too cocky."

Sara wanted to applaud. So far the performance was masterful.

"One more dive," Professor Thorne announced to his audience. "If it's another bust, we go back to the drawing board and figure out where we went wrong."

"Don't worry, Dad." Kurt put his hand on his father's arm. "We'll figure it out, one way or another."

"I guess everyone back in the water." Abigail Thorne waved her arms toward the stern.

Kenny bit down hard on his back teeth, the tension in his jaw clearly visible. He pulled out a dive slate and wrote quietly: *Don't want you going back down.*

Taking the slate away from him, Sara wrote back: *Can't dive alone. Suspicious if I stay.*

She could see him weighing the situation. Finally, he nodded and wrote: *Stay close. Very close.*

For the next forty five minutes, they swam yards away from the location of the overnight damage. Every so often, Chloe would pull out her camera and snap a picture. They filled a bag with some miscellaneous bits of rock when Sara noticed Chloe freeze. Sara took a look around, wondering what had she seen. When Kurt eased to her side and his head jerked up, Sara knew something was up. Chloe started snapping photos like a photographer at a Paris fashion shoot.

Too curious to resist, she signaled for Kenny to follow her. When she reached the siblings it took her a long while to figure out what had gotten them so excited, and then she realized, the rock encrusted formation underneath them wasn't rock, it was cannons. They'd found their wreck.

Now getting that assist overseeing the site was even more crucial than before. Chloe and Kurt ascended first, Kenny and Sara just behind them. Unable to say a word about the find, everyone did their best to pretend it was another unsuccessful effort, when Chloe spun around frantically. "No."

Her father's brow furrowed. Heads turned, no one quite sure if this was more acting.

Her back to the water between them and the other ship, she whispered, "My camera. I must have dropped it."

"I'll get it." Kenny's voice left no room for argument. He was already reaching for a fresh air tank.

Sara moved to do the same.

"You're staying on the boat." Kenny spoke more sharply than usual.

"Nope." Hands on her hips, doing her best to state her case and keep up the farce of not knowing they were being watched. "I don't care if it's just a few minutes to retrieve a dropped item; you never dive alone, ever. You know that."

He stared at her, the muscle in his jaw working. Her logic was unassailable, rooted in the same safety protocols that had been drilled into him for two decades. Finally, he gave a single, sharp nod. "You stay within arm's reach. No exceptions."

"Wouldn't dream of doing anything else."

The second descent was fast and urgent. They dropped straight down, bypassing the scenic route, their focus singular: find the camera. There it was, near a small cluster of fans its dark casing half-buried, almost invisible.

Kenny reached for it. As he secured the camera to a clip on his BCD, Sara turned. Hidden in the shadow of a large coral overhang, not more than ten yards away, were two divers. Unfamiliar divers. They must have slipped into the water from the far side of their boat while everyone's attention was elsewhere. Kenny saw them a second later. His entire posture changed, from relaxed to coiled steel. He signaled to her—stay put, stay behind me.

He swam toward them, not aggressively, but with a clear, deliberate motion that said I see you. The site is not unattended. It happened fast. Startled, the larger of the two lunged, not with fists, but with a long, wicked-looking dive knife he pulled from a sheath on his leg. He came straight at Kenny.

The shock of it almost had her losing her regulator as her mouth threatened to open and scream. Thoughts raced through her mind; did she rush up, ignore safety speeds, and seek help from Kurt or Billy, or, did she do something herself. But what? There was no force under water and those two thugs were bigger than her.

Kenny was already in a wrestling match with the first guy, his hand manacled around the arm that held the knife. All she had to do was sneak up behind the bad guy, except, for a fleeting moment she'd forgotten there were two of them. Where had the other one…

She felt the grip around her ankle. *Shit*. How had she lost sight of him? Spinning around she did her best to kick her leg free. Whether it was adrenaline, desperation, or sheer dumb luck she had no idea, but she managed to break free.

Now Kenny had done the same and was speeding toward her, the other guy on his heels. What a blasted mess.

Arms flailing, doing her best to distract, she spun about, reaching for her own knife, flinging herself back around, she managed to catch her assailant off guard and slashed at his suit. He was close enough for her to see the shock in his eyes. Taking advantage of the moment, she swung again, this time nicking his air hose. The man would have no choice but to surface before he lost all his air.

Just as Kenny reached her, the assailant signaled his partner. In a tumbled blur, Kenny turned on the first guy, reaching for the knife as the man kicked away from him. Undeterred, Kenny grabbed at his leg. The guy swung at him with jerky, frantic motions. The shiny edge of the knife whizzed past Kenny and then with a good last kick, the thug broke free and swam away with his partner in crime. Sara saw a brief, bright ribbon of red cloud the water near Kenny's bicep—a small nick.

Kenny turned to her, his eyes blazing. He gave her a frantic, head-to-toe visual scan. She gave him a thumbs-up, her own adrenaline making her hand tremble. He pointed to his arm, then gave another thumbs-up and signaled for them to ascend.

She nodded, turning to begin their slow journey back to the light when another shadow cut through the cool water. Not again. Mentally preparing for another confrontation, the shadow came into focus and the regulator suddenly felt huge and clumsy in her mouth. Her hand flew to her mask as a gasp she couldn't voice seized her lungs—shark!

CHAPTER FIFTEEN

For a single, precious second after the thugs fled, a wave of pure relief washed over Kenny. Sara was safe. His mind quickly catalogued the next steps: ascend, report, regroup. Then he spotted her frozen in the water, her hand pressed to her mask, her eyes wide with a terror that he feared had nothing to do with the men who had just attacked them. He followed her gaze and his blood ran cold.

It wasn't just a shark. It was a tiger, and a big one—at least twelve feet of slate-gray muscle and prehistoric menace. It moved with an unnerving, fluid grace, its blunt head swinging from side to side as it tested the water. Kenny knew exactly what it was doing. It had scented his blood, a faint but irresistible invitation in the current.

Every ounce of his SEAL training, every instinct honed over twenty years of survival, screamed to life. His mind became a steel trap of tactical assessment. Threat: apex predator. Location: open water, twenty feet below the surface. Asset to protect: Sara. Primary objective: get her out of the water. Now.

Moving to place his body between Sara and the shark, he grabbed her arm, his grip firm, trying to communicate urgency without inducing panic. He pointed emphatically toward the surface, his expression grim. Go. Now.

To his chagrin, she shook her head, her eyes locked on him, on the small, steady stream of blood still trickling from the gash on his bicep. She understood. The shark wasn't interested in her. It was interested in him. And she wasn't leaving him.

Blasted woman. Her courage was going to get them both killed. The shark stopped circling. It turned, its movements no longer curious but deliberate. It was closing the distance.

Kenny's mind raced. Don't act like prey. Don't splash. Don't flee. He drew his knife, not as a weapon to kill—that was a fool's game—but as a tool of defense. A last resort. He pulled Sara behind him, positioning her back-to-back with him. They were a single, larger entity now. Harder to attack.

"Stay with me," his words a useless rumble through his regulator. "Watch my six."

He faced the shark, keeping his eyes locked on it, making himself as big as possible. The tiger shark swam closer, its dark, unblinking eye a void of predatory focus. It was ten feet away. Then eight. He could see the faint stripes on its flank, the raw power in the sweep of its tail.

His heart hammered against his ribs, a frantic drumbeat against the steady hiss of his regulator. This was a different kind of fear. In combat, you could predict an enemy's moves, exploit their tactics. This was primal. Unpredictable. He was no longer a Senior Chief. He was just a man in the water, facing something that had ruled this domain for millions of years.

The shark lunged. Not a full-on attack, but a test. A bump. It came in fast, its massive head aimed at his side. Kenny shoved off the reef floor, using the momentum to swing himself and Sara out of its direct path. The shark's rough, sandpaper-like skin scraped against his leg, a brutal, abrasive impact that sent a jolt through his entire body.

He regained his balance, turning to face it again. He had to keep Sara safe. The shark circled back, now more agitated. Kenny's blood was a stronger scent in the water. He needed to stop the bleeding. Pressing his free hand hard against the gash on his arm, he tried to staunch the flow, risking a glance back at Sara. Her face was pale, but her eyes were clear and focused. She wasn't panicking. And then he heard it.

CLANG. CLANG. CLANG.

Brilliant. Sara had used her knife to bang against the tanks. The sharp, metallic sound vibrated through the water, loud and unnatural. A classic diver's trick to get attention, but in this context, a weapon of auditory warfare. The effect on the shark was immediate. It flinched, its head jerking to the side as the alien sound hit. Its smooth, circling pattern broke. The beast became hesitant, confused by the aggressive, rhythmic noise. It was no longer dealing with silent, bleeding prey; it was facing a loud, unpredictable opponent.

This was their chance. Their only chance. Grabbing hold of Sara, pulling her with him as he kicked powerfully toward the surface, he didn't bother to look back. There was no time to check if the shark was following. There was only the light, the promise of air and safety, and the desperate, all-consuming need to get Sara on that boat.

They broke the surface in a chaotic explosion of foam and saltwater. Adrenaline pumping through his veins, he spied Billy at the rail and the Thornes scrambling, pointing. The world was a blur of motion and shouting. He shoved Sara toward the dive ladder, his arm hooked around her waist.

"Climb!" his voice a guttural command.

He stayed in the water, his body a shield, his eyes scanning the churning surface, knife still in hand. He wouldn't be safe until she was. Not till she scrambled up the ladder did he risk a look down. A dark, massive shape was rising from the depths directly beneath him. Time was running out. Swiftly, he launched himself out of the water, grabbing the lowest rung of the ladder just as a pair of jaws, lined with rows of serrated death, snapped shut on the very spot where his fins had been a split second before. The power of the impact sent a shudder through the entire boat as the shark slammed into the hull, then twisted and disappeared back into the blue.

Kenny hauled himself over the rail, collapsing onto the deck, his chest heaving, his body humming with an overdose of adrenaline. He rolled over, his first and only thought for Sara. She was there, kneeling beside him, her hands hovering over him, her face a mask of terror and relief.

The world narrowed to her face, to her wide, tear-filled eyes. The shark, the thugs, the treasure—it all vanished. There was only this woman, who had faced down a man with a knife and a tiger shark at his back, and hadn't left his side. He reached up, his hand shaking, and cupped her cheek. "You are amazing."

The way her heart beat pounded in her ears, she could barely think, never mind hear. "I thought I was going to lose you."

"Back at you." Swallowing hard, he reached up and pulled her toward him until she practically collapsed on top of him. "I have sacrificed a great deal in my lifetime to keep my team safe, but I have never been as scared of losing anyone as I was down there of losing you."

"Thank you."

"For what? You saved us."

Her cheeks tugged at the corner of her lips. This man was so cute when he was being obtuse. "For caring."

"Caring?" He pulled her impossibly closer. "Sara, I don't just care, I love you."

Loved her? Her mouth fell slightly opened and she quickly snapped it shut. Surely she'd misheard or maybe he meant love you the way he loved the Everretts or the Harpers.

"Don't look so surprised. We might have started this for all the wrong reasons, but loving you is the most right thing I've ever done."

There it was again. The L word. And it didn't sound anything like the affection a man had for his friends. Forcing her lips to move, she finally managed to say, "You're serious."

He nodded.

"Not part of the game?"

"Not a game."

Could it possibly be true? Could she be dreaming?

Could she have lost her mind? Or maybe the shark had killed them both and this was heaven?

Taking her hand from his side, he placed it on his chest, over his heart. "I'm dead serious. Sara Alani, I love you, and I only ask that you give me a chance to convince you that I'm worth taking a chance on, not for show, but for real."

Resisting the urge to pinch herself, she decided instead to go with the flow. If this was a dream, or heaven, what harm could it do to tell him what she felt. "I don't need time."

For a split second she saw the hope in his gaze fade.

"I already love you for real."

A broad smile took over his face and before she could say another word, he pulled her all the way down against him and captured her mouth with his in a kiss that was already curling her toes. She would have gladly stayed right here, kissing Kenny Yates until the cows came home, except the deep sound of a throat clearing reminded her that they had an audience.

Pushing herself to an upright position, she looked up at the group of people surrounding them, all smiling like the Cheshire cat.

Arms crossed, Billy's grin was the widest. "If you two would like some privacy, we could all jump overboard and take our chances with the sharks."

"Sorry." Her cheeks warm with embarrassment, she pushed to her feet. "I, uh, guess we need to report the poachers to the police."

"Already done." The professor held up the camera that he'd taken from Kenny. "Seems the camera snapped a few shots of the idiots attacking you two. I don't think they'll be a problem anymore."

"What about Vance?" Kenny asked, now standing beside her.

Billy sighed. "That might be a little more difficult, but I'm willing to wager the shop that once Vance finds out the police have picked up his hired goons, he and his ship with all his fancy equipment will hightail it out of here to prey on some other shipwreck."

"I don't like the idea of that character getting away with this." Mrs. Thorne frowned at them.

"Well," Billy smiled, "I'm sure he'll get what's coming to him. One way or another."

"I hope sooner than later," the professor added.

The way Billy kept smiling, she had a suspicion that he knew something he wasn't sharing yet.

"Oh, and while I have your attention, Mom was at the shop when I called to update Nick. You're all expected at dinner tonight. But I'd better warn you, she has mistletoe hanging everywhere. And I mean everywhere."

Kenny slid his arm around her waist and pulled her up close against him. His gaze leveled with hers, he smiled down at her. "Not a problem. Not a problem at all."

CHAPTER SIXTEEN

For Sara the scent of roasting kalua pig, plumeria, and pine needles that filled the air of the Everett home would forever smell like Christmas Eve. In the entryway of the house, Kenny's hand warm and solid in hers, she took in the loving chaos unfolding in front of them. Maile easily orchestrated the Christmas Eve feast with the same military precision she'd used for the cookie baking party, and every other major family event.

Across the room, Nick Harper, looking every bit the proud father, bounced his and Kara's youngest on his hip while their son, Bradley, now a blur of perpetual motion, chased Billy and Angela's kids, through the living room. The shrieks of laughter were the party's joyful soundtrack.

Sara's gaze drifted toward Doug Hamilton, his arm slung casually around Emily's shoulders as they stood talking with Emily's sister, Ava, and her husband. Emily's hand rested on her growing baby bump, a serene smile on her face. It seemed like only yesterday that Maile and her own mother had tried to set her up with Doug, a futile effort when it was so clear to everyone that he only had eyes for Emily. Now, looking at them, so happy and settled, Sara felt a wave of pure, uncomplicated joy for her dearest friend.

This was her *ohana*, the family she had chosen. A sprawling, ever-expanding network of Navy SEALs, EOD techs, lawyers, teachers, and architects, all woven together by friendship and aloha.

"There you are!" Her mother hurried over, her face beaming. She hugged Sara tightly before turning her attention to Kenny. "I was just telling Maile that you two are the handsomest couple here."

"I think you might be a little biased, Mrs. Alani." Kenny smiled easily at the woman.

Her arms full of serving platters, Maile strolled by. "Missy, your husband is looking for you, and Sara, honey, can you check the kalua pig? It should be just about ready."

Sara moved through the familiar bustle with a sense of calm she rarely enjoyed in these big gatherings. No longer a need to scan for escape routes, no bracing for matchmaking ambushes. She loved being a part of these huge family events, appreciated being treated as if she too were an Everrett.

"Mele Kalikimaka!" Emily appeared at her elbow, carrying a tray of haupia. "You look happy."

"I am happy." Lifting the foil from the pig, Sara breathed in the smoky, tender aroma. "Genuinely happy."

"Good. Because Mom's watching you and Kenny with that satisfied look she gets when one of her plans works out."

Sara glanced toward the living room where Maile was arranging poinsettias around the base of the Christmas tree. "She's going to take full credit for this, isn't she?"

"Absolutely. She and your mother are probably already planning to write a matchmaking manual."

"Need any help in here?" Kenny appeared behind her, his hands steady on her shoulders, his breath warm against her neck. Oh how she loved this real relationship.

"We've got it handled." Emily's eyes twinkled at the way he stood by her friend. "Though you might want to warn the guys that Mom hung mistletoe over every doorway."

Kenny raised an eyebrow. "Every doorway?"

Emily chuckled. "She's been very thorough."

Sara caught Kenny's grin and felt heat rise in her cheeks. Three weeks ago, the thought of mistletoe would have sent her into hiding. Now, she found herself looking forward to the excuse.

Mulling about, hand in hand with Kenny, Sara chatted with Kara for a bit, played pass the baby around from one relative to another, and laughed watching the kids out in the backyard practicing their hula for the elders, the island way of showing respect and love. From somewhere inside, the sound of a strumming ukulele could be heard. All the sights and sounds of a typical Hawaiian Christmas, and she couldn't imagine having it any other way.

"Hey," Nick came up next to Kenny, "I just got off the phone with Brooklyn."

"And?" Kenny asked. Ever since the day of the shark and diver incident, Sara knew that the guys had reached out to their former Navy buddy Luke "Brooklyn" Chapman. The man had apparently not only been a super SEAL, but a member of the CIA and now ran an elite team of investigators and security experts. According to Kenny and Nick, the perfect person to trap Vance.

"Seems our friend Vance got greedy," Nick began.

"Yeah, well," Kenny sighed, "no surprise there.

"With a little help from his friends, and in-laws, Brooklyn's set up a sting operation. They knew Vance was networking to sell the San Isidro's location—or what he thought was the location—to the highest bidding private collector."

Kenny chuckled again. "Let me guess—Brooklyn?"

"Close. Thanks to Brooklyn's connections, an undercover agent with Interpol. They got Vance on a wire transfer, trying to sell treasure he didn't have from a wreck he couldn't find."

Sara couldn't help but laugh. "So the modern-day pirate gets taken down by a con."

"Poetic justice," Kenny agreed. He reached out, his thumb gently brushing a stray strand of hair from her cheek. "Looks like the Thornes will have all the peace and quiet they need to finish their work."

Sara's dad came out of the house, strumming "Mele Kalikimaka" on the ukulele and everything else seemed to stop. The kids came forward to do their hula, and the family and guests all joined in on the singing. From the traditional Hawaiian Christmas song, they moved to singing "White Christmas," and then "Silent Night."

Leaning back against Kenny, the massive Christmas

tree across from them, Sara simply enjoyed the moment. Perfect holiday bliss.

The last notes of "Silent Night" faded into the gentle murmur of the party and the distant whisper of the waves. The kids, exhausted from their hula performance, were finally starting to wind down, their heads drooping on their parents' shoulders. Kenny stood with Sara, his arm around her, feeling the solid warmth of her pressed against his side. The contentment he felt was so profound, so complete, it was terrifying. He'd spent two decades chasing the adrenaline of the mission, never realizing that this quiet, steady peace was the true prize.

Now came the hardest part. The final mission.

His heart, which had remained steady while facing down terrorists, combatants, and even tiger sharks, began to hammer against his ribs. He could lead a SEAL team through a hostile insertion, but planning for a life with Sara felt like jumping out of an airplane without a parachute.

"Hey," he murmured, his voice rougher than he'd intended. "Can you come with me for a minute? There's something I want to show you."

She looked up at him, her green eyes questioning but full of trust. "Of course."

He led her by the hand, away from the warm glow of Maile's house, past the tiki torches lighting the garden path, and out to the front yard. Opening the door to the backseat of his car, he reached in and pulled out a large rolled up sheet of paper. Taking hold of Sara's slender fingers in his free hand, he led her to the front of the car and letting go of her, slowly spread the paper out across the hood.

"What's this?"

"A map of the island. More specifically, these areas here are the ones of interest." He pointed to a penciled circle about the mountainside land he owned.

"That's your land?" Her smile beamed up at him.

"Yes." He nodded. It gave him an unexpected burst of pleasure that she remembered and recognized his lands. Taking in a deep breath, here went nothing. "As you know, when I first arrived, I had no idea where I would land permanently."

She bobbed her head and for a second, he noticed some of the sparkle dimmed in her gaze.

"Pretty much, within the first week of our little ruse, I had figured out that regardless of what happened between us, Kona would be my home now."

Her gaze remained wary.

He let out a short, unsteady laugh. "More precisely, somewhere between a scavenger hunt and getting humbled by a surfboard, my objective became clearer."

A hint of hope lit in her eyes.

"My entire adult life has been about following charts like this to a mission objective. A place I was ordered to go. This is the first chart I've ever made where the destination is a choice."

"Choices are nice." Her smile seemed awfully fragile. "I haven't always felt as though I had many. At least not in recent years."

He thought of all the double shifts she'd worked, putting her life on hold, all for the dream of a place to call her own. Reaching out, his hand covered hers where it rested on the map, the paper cool beneath their skin. "That changes now. For both of us." He tapped the penciled circle again, the land on the mountainside. "This is the only spot on the island I want to build a life. But I have no idea how to do it. I can plan an op in a hostile country down to the last second, but ask me about floor plans or where the kitchen should go to get the best morning sun... I'm completely lost."

She gave a half-hearted chuckle. "I can't picture you lost. Ever."

That made one of them. Leveling his gaze with hers, he sucked in a deep breath and prayed he wasn't making a terrible miscalculation. "I'm not asking for forever. It's too soon. I'm just asking for... your help. Your expertise. I know you've been dreaming of your own place for years. You probably know more about what makes a house a home than anyone I've ever met." He took a breath, burying the nerves threatening to steal his words. "I want to build a home up there. And I don't want to do it without you. Be my partner in this mission. Help me plan it. And maybe... if we're both still here when the foundation is poured and the walls go up... maybe we can see about making some more dreams come true."

Waiting, watching, praying, he saw the second the fragility in her smile bloomed into a radiant, tear-filled warmth that seemed to outshine the moon. She squeezed his hand, her touch sending a jolt of pure relief through him. "So, you're saying you need a partner for a long-term planning operation?" A playful, teasing light returned to her eyes.

"The most important one of my life."

"Well." She leaned in, her lips just inches from his, her warm breath ghosting across his skin. "I think I know a girl who would be perfect for the job."

He didn't need any more encouragement than that. Lowering his head, he captured her mouth with his, a kiss that wasn't a proposal or a promise, but a simple, profound agreement. A beginning. When he finally pulled back, he rested his forehead against hers, the crinkle of the map a soft sound between them. "So," he murmured against her lips, "first order of business for the planning committee?"

"We are definitely going to need a very big porch," she whispered back, her smile evident in her voice. "For watching the sunset."

He laughed, a sound full of a future he could finally see, a future built on a shared plan. He pulled her tight against him, the map of their future held fast between them. He wasn't adrift anymore. He was home. "Merry Christmas, Sara Alani."

"Merry Christmas, Kenny Yates."

Enjoy an excerpt from
Sweet Beginnings

P reston Sweet slammed the door of his SUV and slipped his keys into his pocket. Unlike his apartment in town, the front door of the Sweet Ranch was never locked. From the near empty drive, it looked like only his brother Carson had beat him home. Every Sunday the driveway would be filled with cars. Tonight would be the first time the house would be bursting with Sweets on a weeknight for no other reason than his mom had called and asked.

The sound of spitting gravel cut off his thoughts. Even with the dust cloud blowing in the thick summer air, preventing a clear view of the approaching car, he knew the driver had to be Rachel. His sister was the only person in the family who considered every open road a NASCAR track.

The car came to a screeching halt within a few feet of him, though it felt like inches. She probably should have moved to Hollywood and been a stunt car driver. "Cutting it pretty close, don't you think?"

Rachel yanked her overnight bag from the back seat and shook her head at her brother. "Nah. I had plenty of room."

Even though he had just seen her a couple of weeks ago, he scooped her into a warm hug as though it had been forever ago.

"Any idea what this is all about?" she mumbled into his shoulder. The same underlying tinge of tension he'd felt since his mom's cryptic call could be felt in Rachel's embrace.

He shook his head and eased back. "I can't decide if Mom announcing she's getting married would be best-case scenario or worst-case scenario."

Like a shot, Rachel sprang back. "Mom's getting married? I thought you didn't know what this is all about."

"That's not what I meant." He shook his head more forcefully. "I was simply wondering what could be so important that she would call all of us and tell us she needed us home. *Now*. Then it hit me a wedding would be something seriously important. Especially if it was *our* mother getting married again. Once my mind wandered that far, then I couldn't decide if that would be a relief or the beginning of some new kind of hell."

"She's not even dating." Rachel smacked him lightly on the arm and growled her frustration with her big brother. "Why would you even go there?"

"Because the other option was she's dying and I don't want to go there—*ever*."

On a heavy sigh, Rachel nodded. "That would certainly make getting hitched more appealing."

He reached for her bag. "Did you ever think about it?"

"Mom getting married again?"

Moving forward, he bobbed his head.

"Nope." She fell into step beside him. "I just can't picture anyone with Mom except Dad."

"Know what you mean, but still, it has to be pretty lonely some days in this big old house."

"Yeah." She stopped at the porch steps and looked up at the expanse of the beloved two-story stone and log home that had grown through the generations to house the Sweet family for well over two hundred years. "But for now, I don't think this is it."

"I hope not. I'm not ready to think about Mom remarrying. Some day, but not yet." Preston held the door open for his sister, the way his dad had drummed into all their heads since they were old enough to walk. "And the more I think about this call, the more I'm sure whatever it is, I'm not going to like it either."

"Any word from Garret?" Rachel strolled past him.

"No, and I didn't expect to hear back from our nature-loving brother. He warned us there's no cell service where he and his buddies are camping in Idaho."

"I know." His sister shrugged. "I just thought, sometimes with technology you never know."

Despite the massive appearance from the outside of the home, the inside was cozy, welcoming with large upholstered furniture that created a comfy seating area with a great view of the expansive property, and quiet. Too quiet.

Rachel paused mid-stride. "I'm surprised Mom isn't here waiting for us."

The same thing had crossed Preston's mind. For as long as he could remember, since the day he'd left home for college, the minute his mom heard the rumble of his engine, she was out the door and on the porch waving frantically at him. As a matter of fact, now that he thought about it, everything inside and out seemed unusually quiet.

"Maybe she's helping the ranch hands with something. This is around vaccine time before the big sales."

"Maybe." Without being given direction, he led his sister down the hall to the room she'd shared with her twin Jillian, and dropped the bag on the bed. "I'm going to see if I can find Carson and Mom."

"I saw a light on in the study." Rachel unzipped her bag. "I'm going to take a minute and unpack."

"Don't you usually pack a lot less?"

She shrugged. "Since I'm mostly working from home, I figured no harm in planning to stay a few extra days."

The thought to pack a bag and turn a midweek supper into a very long weekend had occurred to him as well, but then he decided that first, he had enough clothing still at the house to last him a month, and second, showing up for an extended stay might fall in the camp of overreacting to a simple call for a family dinner in the middle of the week. "That'll make Mom happy."

His sister flashed a huge toothy grin. "I know."

"Women," he muttered, laughing to himself. After four boys, and nothing but male cousins, the birth of twin girls had been a delightful surprise. That kid and his other sister had everyone in the family wrapped around their fingers from the day they were born, and he doubted that would ever change.

Retreating down the hall, he turned into his father's

domain. Charles Sweet's study hadn't changed much since the days when Preston and his siblings had trotted around on wooden pony sticks with makeshift lassos and pretended to rope everything from the toy horses to the desktop lamp—and each other. In an effort to keep them all in one piece, their father had dutifully uttered the occasional warning of 'be careful' or 'not so rough'—most likely for their mother's benefit. More so though, their dad had simply done his best to get through the paperwork part of the ranch business while his children created havoc around him.

Funny, in all the time since they'd buried their father, the familiar scent of his aftershave seemed to still linger in the air. Or perhaps it was nothing more than memories and wishful thinking.

"Did Mom tell anyone why we're all here?" Carson uncapped the crystal decanter behind the desk then raised an empty glass to his brother.

"No, thanks." Preston waved off the silent invitation. "Rachel is unpacking. Neither of us has any idea what this is all about."

Carson, who since their father's passing had done his best to step up in their oldest brother Kade's absence and quietly be there for their mother, sank heavily in one of the oversized leather chairs, swirled the ice in the two fingers of bourbon, and took a long swallow.

"Looks like you've had a hard day." Preston took a seat across from him, leaving the sofa and a smaller chair for his mom and siblings.

"Hard week." Carson eyed the glass glimmering from the reflection of the nearby lamp. "Heck, more like weeks."

Hands threaded in front of him, Preston leaned forward. Even though Carson was the most private of the siblings, Preston couldn't remember seeing his brother stew so sternly over anything. "What's wrong?"

"Just another day in the flip world." Carson sighed. "Turns out the most recent project we sank all our available cash into, is now knee deep in litigation."

"That's something new."

"For me it is. Seems all the houses in that subdivision are in a class action suit against the original developers and we can't do squat until it's settled. My ninety-day rehab schedule just went down the drain."

"So now what?"

"Not sure. I'm okay for a while, but the reno budget is growing tighter every day until I come up with a plan B."

"Sorry, man." Preston changed his mind about that drink after all.

The loose board by the threshold squeaked, announcing his sister's arrival. "A little early to be drinking, isn't it?"

"What's that saying, it's five o'clock somewhere?" Carson leaned forward and set his drink on the table then looked at his watch. "It's been five o'clock on the east coast for over half an hour."

"In that case," Rachel smiled up at Preston still at the bar, "make mine on the rocks."

"Aren't you too young to drink?" Carson teased.

His sister flashed a wistful grin. "Oh, to be twenty-one again."

"Twenty-one? Aren't you sixteen?"

"Here we go again." Rachel accepted her glass and rolled her eyes at her brothers.

Didn't matter how old she grew, in their eyes she and Jillian would always be the kid sisters who needed their big bad brothers to keep them safe and out of trouble, especially since the two had been stubborn and strong-willed since birth. Not even falling from the boys' tree house and breaking an arm had taken the edge off of Rachel's adventurous streak.

"Never mind that." Preston figured the least he could do was reel in his brother's sense of humor, especially since they had more pressing matters at hand. Setting his drink aside, he slid his phone from his pocket and hit his mom's number.

"Mom?" Rachel asked.

Preston nodded, and Carson scooted to the edge of his seat, carefully watching the phone, then sliding back when the call went to voice mail.

Still staring at the now quiet phone, Rachel frowned. "Anyone else starting to feel guilty for making Mom worry when we missed curfew and forgot our phones?"

"Not me." Preston smiled. "I was perfect."

Rachel rolled her eyes at him and then her face stiffened. "Seriously, maybe we should make some phone calls. Friends, Ray, make sure she's all right."

"She's a grown woman who has worked this ranch for longer than any of us have been alive, and running it just fine without Dad. I'm sure she'll be here any minute and laugh off our concerns." Carson's words painted a picture of a calm, unconcerned son, but the look in his gaze and leaving a drink unfinished spoke volumes to just how concerned he was about their mother's tardiness. What in heaven's name could she be up to?

"Loud noise reactivity. Perceived confrontation. German Shepherd. What time?" Sarah Sue Conroy tapped the pad she'd used to scribble data on the most recent dog needing to be homed. Even with years of experience as the foster coordinator for a non-profit military canine organization, thanks to an onslaught of military working dogs recently coming through the system, her usual sources for fosters were growing slim. There had to be an answer and she'd better find it before Tuesday morning at zero nine hundred hours when this poor boy's last chance for being homed ran out. A few more details and requisite polite exchange of weather, family, and allergy season, and she disconnected the call, bringing her laptop screen to life.

"I have to run." Her father grabbed a protein bar off the counter and shoved it in his jacket pocket, then casually pilfered one, then two, of the chocolate chip cookies she'd made earlier in the day. "Mary Mahoney has finally gone into labor for real."

"Finally?" Sarah had been daughter to a country doctor long enough, and spent enough summers playing receptionist and aide to know almost as much about medicine as her father—though every med school in the world would probably disagree with her. Still, even she knew that every pregnant woman eventually had a baby.

"She's ten days overdue and every time Braxton Hicks start she'd be in my office convinced this was *the* time."

"How do you know this isn't another false alarm?" As sure as she knew her name was Sarah Sue Conroy, she knew there would be a definitive answer.

"Heard it in her voice."

And *that* was why her dad was so very good at what he did. She still remembered the time that Mrs. Harper had called to tell the doc that she was having strong twinges and was going to climb into the tub to relax before the main event. When her husband called back an hour later in a panic, her father told him to hold the phone close to his wife's face so Sarah's father could listen. A few long moments later and the well-loved old doctor informed Mr. Harper not to wait for him, but rather to take his wife to the hospital and don't worry about the speed limits, the sheriff would understand. An hour later, Faith Harper was born.

Her father paused long enough to kiss her on the temple. "It's nice to have you back. Not much about the chaos in today's world I'm happy about, but at least one good thing has come from it. If the business world's acceptance of folks working from home means having you here instead of Austin, then it's a welcome change. Love you."

"Love you too. And it's nice to be back." In the half a dozen years since she'd moved to Austin, she hadn't realized just how much she missed living in a sleepy town. Apparently, she missed it all a lot. A whole lot of lot. Especially chatting over dinner about anything from Mildred McEntire's latest bedazzled outfit, to who'd won that day's corn hole match at the park, to the latest fight at the town council over their beloved town of Honeysuckle, Texas. Nary a week went by when there wasn't a disagreement of some kind between the faction who wanted to promote the honeysuckle arts and crafts that filled the Main Street shops with everything from candles to potpourri, and the faction who felt being corn hole capital of Texas was the bigger advantage for promotion dollars. But if her new working arrangements panned out, fingers crossed, maybe, just maybe, she could move home for good.

"Odds are I'll be home late." Her dad stood at the open front door. "First babies usually take their sweet time. If I am, you go ahead and take the casserole out of the oven and invite yourself over to the Sweets. Alice would probably enjoy the company. Even though it's been over a year, she's still a bit out of sorts over losing Charlie, not that she realizes it." He pressed his lips into a thin line and shook his head with a sigh. "Anyhow, company would do her good."

"Will do!"

The front door closed in the distance and Sarah pushed to her feet. A casserole dinner with Miss Alice would be way more fun than eating alone, waiting for her dad to come home. Besides, she hadn't seen any of the Sweets since Charlie's funeral. It was a miserable reason to come home and she'd barely had any chance to say more than "I'm sorry for your loss" to the people who had been like a second family to her for most of her life. Maybe she could even dig up a bottle of Abigail Fine's honeysuckle wine to go with dinner.

According to the oven clock, dinner would be ready in thirty minutes. Enough time for her to get a little work done. Alice Sweet had done such a great job with her son's dog, maybe she would have a few suggestions for Sarah. She'd opened a new browser and watched the swirly thing spin when another thought smacked her upside the head. Why not ask Ms. Alice if she would be willing to take on another troubled dog? After all, if she was left alone to rattle around in the big house, a new dog could be just the ticket. That is if Brady and the foster could share Alice and the house. It was the perfect solution really. Therapeutic companionship for everyone. Yes. The more she thought about it the more she was sure this would be the answer she needed. Now all she had to do was convince Alice Sweet.

Fake Dating the SEAL is available now

MEET CHRIS

USA TODAY Bestselling Author of dozens of contemporary novels, including the award winning Aloha Series, Chris Keniston lives in suburban Dallas with her husband, two human children, and two canine children. Though she loves her puppies equally, she admits being especially attached to her German Shepherd rescue. After all, even dogs deserve a happily ever after.

More on Chris and all her books can be found at
www.chriskeniston.com

Follow Chris' Monday Blog at her website
ChrisKenistonAuthor

Follow Chris on Facebook at
ChrisKenistonAuthor

Never miss a New Release!
Sign up for News from Chris:
www.chriskeniston.com/newsletter.html

Questions? Comments?
I would love to hear from you! You can reach me at:
chris@chriskeniston.com